X

STORM OVER WYOMING

STORM OVER WYOMING

by

Jack Edwardes

Dales Large Print Books
Long Preston, North Yorkshire,
BD23 4ND, England.

British Library Cataloguing in Publication Data.

Edwardes, Jack
    Storm over Wyoming.

A catalogue record of this book is
available from the British Library

ISBN   978-1-84262-650-4 pbk

First published in Great Britain 2007 by Robert Hale Limited

Copyright © Jack Edwardes 2007

Cover illustration © Gordon Crabb by arrangement with
Alison Eldred

The right of Jack Edwardes to be identified as the author of this
work has been asserted by him in accordance with the
Copyright, Designs and Patents Act, 1988

Published in Large Print 2008 by arrangement with
Robert Hale Limited

Dales Large Print is an imprint of Library Magna Books Ltd.

Printed and bound in Great Britain by
T.J. (International) Ltd., Cornwall, PL28 8RW

CHAPTER ONE

Luke Stafford was maybe five or six miles from Storm Creek when he heard the shot. His right hand moved to the butt of his Navy Colt, his lean body tense as he stared hard towards the bend in the trail. In the rooming-house where he'd stayed a couple of nights back there'd been talk of trouble around Storm Creek. A corn-merchant told of a killing, and folks being driven away from their homes. Stafford reckoned he'd had enough trouble these past months to last him for a while. He wasn't looking for more.

The shot came from about 500 yards away, he judged, from a sidearm or maybe from a small calibre long gun, its sound muffled by trees. His eyes remained fixed ahead while he shortened the rein of his palomino allowing his pack horse to close up.

The two animals slowed to a walk and came to a halt. Stafford sat easy in the saddle, watchful, his ears cocked for any sound that might give him some notion of what had caused the gunshot. From over the lake to the east came the honking of wild geese. The light wind ruffled the leaves of the cotton-woods that prevented him from seeing further along the trail.

Maybe the gunshot was nothing more than some youngster out target-shooting or after jack-rabbits. He'd learned at the stage station that few folks used this trail into Storm. The wider trail beyond the lake was more favoured by stagecoach drivers and merchants shipping goods in wagons.

But caution had kept him alive doing dangerous work, and he wasn't minded to throw it to the wind. The letter he'd received from the bank back East a couple of months ago showed he was being smart with his money. He meant to live long enough to spend it.

He eased the Navy from its holster and rested the heavy sidearm on his thigh before touching his heels to the palomino's sides. When he rounded the bend, the Navy now loose by his leg, he saw a bare-headed young man, in his mid-twenties, a couple of hun-dred yards away. Stafford's grip tightened on the Navy's butt as he saw the young man held a sidearm down by his side.

A hat lay crumpled on the ground a few yards from where he stood, and Stafford guessed he'd been thrown into the dirt. From the stillness of the roan which lay on the ground, Stafford guessed the young stranger had just shot the animal. Stafford walked the palomino forward, the grip on the butt of his Navy relaxing as he saw the stranger slide his sidearm into its holster and raise his head to look in Stafford's direction.

'Howdy, stranger,' Stafford called.

He slid his own sidearm back into its holster. When he got nearer to the dead animal he saw the cheek of the young man's face was bloody, the side of his neck and his hands badly scratched. There were smudges of dirt on his good clothes and a tear in his leather trail jacket.

'Stafford's the name. You all in one piece?'

He slid easily from the saddle, bringing the reins over the palomino's head. The pack horse moved alongside, and after briefly nuzzling at each other's necks, both animals lowered their heads to nibble at the bunch and buffalo grass.

'Reckon so, mister.' The young man kicked out in frustration at the dead horse. 'The name's Frank Brand. I'm sure glad you came along.' Brand lifted his shoulders. 'Dumb sonovabitch trod in a jack-rabbit hole an' broke his leg. I coulda been walkin' a long time.'

'I'll lend a hand,' Stafford said. 'My pack horse is strong an' he'll carry you and your rig into Storm Creek. If we move ourselves we'll be there by noon.' He looked around him. 'Get your hat. It's a mite fancy to be in the dirt.'

Without waiting for the young man to reply Stafford dropped to one knee by the carcass of the roan and began to loosen the saddle strings. Brand's saddle bore fancy designs. The youngster was well-heeled that was for sure. Stafford had noticed a similar design traced on the gleaming leather of his boots. He was slipping the latigo through the rigging ring when Brand spoke behind him.

'I ain't got time to go back to Storm,' he said. 'How much will you take for your palomino? I got plenty of cash. An' your pack horse'll carry you to Storm.'

Stafford looked over his shoulder. There was a note of desperation in the young man's voice. Had he been older and rougher looking, and in different clothes, Stafford might have thought he was running from something.

'My mount ain't for sale,' he said. 'There'll

be good horses in town, I reckon. You'll get another without trouble. You ain't gonna lose much time.'

'I ain't goin' back!' Brand's voice rose almost to a shout. 'Mister, I'll give you twice what your horse is worth.' He thrust his hand into the pocket of his leather trail coat and pulled out a wad of bills. 'Here. The money's yourn.'

Stafford stood up slowly. Maybe the young man's fall had shaken him up more than he realized. He sure was acting as if he had ants in his pants.

'Now take it easy, feller,' he said quietly. 'An' don't go flashin' that bankroll at folks or some mean critter's gonna take it off you.' He frowned, his eye on the wad of bills. That was a heap of money for a young man to be carrying. Maybe, after all, he'd got the wrong notion about Brand.

'I hope you ain't runnin' from any law.'

'No, I ain't runnin' from the law!' Brand turned his head to look away from Stafford in the direction of the far horizon. 'I'd be better fixed if that's all it was,' he said, the sudden bitterness in his voice surprising Stafford.

'Then all you're gonna lose is time.' Stafford said. He half-turned back to the dead

11

roan. 'Let's get the rig o' yourn off this critter.'

'Hold it there, mister!'

There was a harsh note in Brand's voice that caused Stafford to jerk his head around. Then he stood very still. The young man, standing with his feet apart, had his arm extended before him, his Smith & Wesson aimed directly at Stafford's head.

'What the hell d'you think you're doin?' Stafford said evenly.

'I'm takin' the palomino, an' you ain't stoppin' me.'

Stafford felt a wave of weariness sweep over him. Was it only two months before that he'd collected his paycheck and told McParlen, his boss, that once the job in Colorado was finished he was going to take some rest? He could remember his exact words. 'I'm gonna take a break from trail trash, guns, and trouble. See an old friend, sit on his porch and drink some whiskey with him.' Now some brat had a bead on him for no good reason.

'You be damned careful what you're doin' with that weapon,' Stafford said. 'An' think what you're doin' afore you steal a man's horse. Folks where I come from hang horse-thieves. I guess they do the same 'round these parts.'

Brand dropped the wad of bills he'd been holding in his left hand. The paper money riffled in the breeze as it fell onto the grass. 'I ain't stealin'. I'm payin' you. You're gettin' more than the horse is worth and you get to take my rig. It's worth two o' yourn.'

Stafford shrugged. 'I ain't sellin'. I'm keepin' both horses an' the rig. So it's thievin'.'

'I ain't got time to argue. Drop your gunbelt an' put your hands in the air!'

Stafford didn't move, inwardly cursing his luck. Had he not spent ten minutes skirting a rock fall earlier that morning he'd have been ten minutes further along the trail. He'd have passed Brand nearer to Storm. They'd have probably wished each other a good day. Maybe even set a fire and taken some coffee together. Now, a jack-rabbit hole and a stupid horse had landed him in this barrel of tar. Stafford blew air through pursed lips.

'You been readin' too much o' Ned Buntline, young feller,' he said.

The Smith & Wesson in Brand's hand kicked and Stafford felt the wind of the slug as it passed his shoulder. An instant later the loud noise of the discharge slammed against his ears. Goddamnit! Muscles tightened across his shoulders and his stomach felt as if a mule had kicked him.

'You crazy young sonovabitch!'

Brand's face was set hard. 'I can use this gun, mister. I tol' you twice I ain't goin' back to Storm. Now loose that gunbelt, an' make it real slow. Then get your hands in the air.'

For a moment they stood still, staring hard at each other. Then with his left hand Stafford slowly unbuckled his belt, the weight of his Navy causing it to drop heavily to the ground.

'Up!' Brand shouted.

Stafford raised his arms, clasping his hands at the nape of his neck.

Satisfied, the young man lowered his weapon and backed away. He took half-a-dozen careful paces, his boots brushing the ground as he felt his way to reach the palomino, his eyes never leaving Stafford.

'You get on that horse,' Stafford said, 'an' there's no goin' back.'

The young man's mouth tightened and he remained silent. His eyes fixed on Stafford, he reached back and fumbled with the leading rein until the pack horse was free. Then he caught hold of the palomino's reins and looped them over the horn. He shifted

14

his feet, preparing to mount, and for an instant he looked down at the stirrup.

The rays of the morning sun glinted on the metal of the knife as it flew through the air between Stafford and Brand. The razor-sharp point sank into Brand's forearm. For an instant Brand stood motionless, his head down, his neck rigid as he stared with bulging eyes at the knife protruding from his limb. The Smith & Wesson slipped from his nerveless fingers and fell to the ground. His head went back and he shattered the silence with his roar of pain.

Stafford took four loping paces. His bunched fist flashed up, sending Brand crashing to the ground like a falling tree in a forest. Stafford kicked away the sidearm towards his own gunbelt before slamming the high heel of his trail boot onto the young man's wrist, prompting more shouts of pain.

'Shut your hollerin'. You ain't gonna die. I oughta make sure you never hold a gun agin.'

He put his weight on Brand's wrist causing the young man to twist on the ground, his eyes wide with fear. Then, as if relenting, Stafford moved his boot, releasing the pressure. He bent forward to snatch the neckerchief from around the young man's throat. Grasping the hilt of his knife, he pulled it steadily from the young man's arm. Blood flowed, darkening the leather of Brand's jacket. Stafford pressed the neckerchief hard against the wound, wrapping the corners around Brand's arm and tying them with a tight knot. After wiping the blade on the grass Stafford reached back to the nape of his neck and pushed the knife beneath his shirt. It slid easily into the soft leather sheath hanging between his shoulder blades on a leather string.

'On your feet!'

Stafford grasped Brand's trail coat by the lapels, heaving him to his feet and dragging him the few yards to where his own gunbelt and the Smith & Wesson lay on the ground. The young man staggered a couple of yards when Stafford shoved him, falling to the ground onto his injured arm, his moans of pain becoming louder. Stafford kept his eyes on him while he buckled on his gunbelt and tucked Brand's sidearm into the top of his trail pants. He stepped forward and again heaved the youngster to his feet.

'Now get on that pack horse. You fall off, an' I'll drag you into Storm. You're gonna spend some time in jail. You get lucky, an' maybe some feller'll ride out for your rig.'

He stood back to watch as Brand climbed awkwardly behind the canvas-covered boxes on the back of the pack horse. His head was down and his injured arm hung loosely by his side. Satisfied that Brand would cause no further trouble Stafford mounted his palomino, and turned the animal's head in the direction of Storm Creek. His mouth twitched. It was a hell of a way to start a visit to an old friend from the War.

CHAPTER TWO

As the two men approached the last bend of the trail that would take them into Storm Creek, Brand spoke for the first time since he'd been forced to mount the pack horse.

'Mr Stafford, I got somethin' to say.'

'Anythin' you got to say you can save for the sheriff,' Stafford barked.

Damn fool youngster sounded as if he was going to try and wheedle his way out of trouble. That shot over his shoulder, or over his head, or whatever Brand had intended, was too close for comfort. A spell in the local jail would teach him to think twice before acting crazy with a sidearm.

Stafford urged his palomino into a gentle trot, anxious now to deliver Brand to the sheriff and be about his own business. The young man began to speak again but then must have realized that Stafford wasn't listening, for his voice trailed away.

Both horses came around the bend and the rough ground of the trail began to give way to the hardpack of Storm Creek's Main

Street. His first sight of the town took Stafford by surprise. Maybe it was the name of the settlement. He'd expected Storm Creek to be a clutch of wooden shacks lined up either side of a dusty track and maybe a few clapboards set back from the noise and bustle for the more prosperous townsfolk.

Instead, Storm Creek was an established small town showing signs of prosperity. Flanking the street were numerous stores. A stagecoach office was marked by a painted sign. A livery stable showed large white letters on the side of a high building. Halfway along the street Stafford could see a painted board announcing the Majestic Hotel. Fifty yards beyond the hotel, a burly man with moustaches, wearing a white apron, was opening the door of the Nugget Saloon. Directly opposite the saloon, a finger post jutted into the street marking the sheriff's office. Stafford hauled in the lead rein of the pack horse a couple of feet bringing Brand closer to him. Walking his palomino, he headed for the middle of Main Street.

Ahead of him townsfolk hurried along the boardwalks intent on their business. Drummers, toting their wares in large carpet bags, criss-crossed the street casting wary eyes at passing cowboys who amused themselves by deliberately riding close to these greenhorns from back East.

Stafford was maybe fifty yards along Main Street when he realized that his arrival had caused a stir. Men, some in city suits, some in dusty coveralls, stopped on the boardwalk to stare in his direction. Women in cheap cotton dresses that barely reached their boots stood alongside others in fancy flowing skirts that brushed the boardwalk, and stared open-mouthed at Stafford's progress. A cowboy appeared from the dry goods store to shout in their direction but Stafford and Brand passed him without responding.

As Stafford halted his palomino at the hitching rail outside the sheriffs office, the door opened and onto the boardwalk stepped the sheriff, maybe fifty years old, his grey moustaches drooping around his mouth, his belly bulging over the belt that supported a Colt Peacemaker on his hip.

The sheriff looked first at Stafford then at Brand, a deep frown topping the puzzled expression in his sharp, intelligent, eyes. His hands dropped to hitch his belt over his belly.

'What the hell's goin' on?'

Stafford stepped down from his mount. He pulled out Brand's sidearm from the top of his pants and mounted the first step to the boardwalk.

'The name's Stafford. Gotta would-be horse-thief for your jail, Sheriff. Damn no-good drew a gun on me. Coulda killed me.'

The sheriff took Brand's sidearm, looking down as if he'd never seen a Smith & Wesson before. He gave a deep sigh, and looked across at Brand who remained silent and unmoving on the pack horse.

'Mr Frank, are you gonna tell me what's been goin' on?'

Stafford's head jerked up to stare at the sheriff. Had he heard aright? Mr Frank? A sheriff who watched his manners with a horse-thief? What the hell was going on here?

'Now wait a while, Sheriff–' Stafford began.

'I'm waitin', Mr Stafford,' the sheriff interrupted. 'I'm waitin' to hear what Mr Frank has to say.' He turned in Brand's direction. 'Go ahead, Mr Frank.'

Then before Brand could reply, the sheriff held up his hand seemingly aware for the first time of the knot of onlookers who had gathered around, all appearing anxious to hear what had caused Mr Frank to be the prisoner of this tall, broad-shouldered stranger.

'You folks! This is law business and none o' yourn. Please go about your day unless you've a mind to spend some time with me.'

The crowd broke up quickly, men stepping smartly away, albeit with lingering expressions of curiosity on their faces as they snatched backward glances at the three men. Satisfied, the sheriff turned again to Brand and nodded.

'OK,' he said. 'Let's hear it.'

'Sheriff Mackay, it was just damn crazy. Me and Mr Stafford got the wrong notion about each other and–'

'Hold on!' Stafford interrupted.

'I tol' you once: you hold on,' Mackay barked. 'I'm listenin' to Mr Frank.'

'My horse broke a leg,' Brand continued. 'I tried to buy Mr Stafford's mount and he musta got the wrong idea 'cos he winged me with a knife.' Brand held up his injured arm. 'That's when I fired a shot over his head, you know, just to calm him down. You know I can use that gun, I wasn't aimin' at him.'

Mackay frowned. 'So how come he's brought you in?'

Brand lowered his eyes. 'I guess I thought that was the end of it until he knocked me to the ground.' He held a hand to the side of his face, now blue from a large bruise.

Mackay sucked noisily on his teeth. 'I'll see you over to Doc Mayerling.' He turned to Stafford and jerked a thumb in the direction of his office. 'I got questions for you, Mr Stafford. Get some coffee, an' I'll be back in five minutes.'

Stafford opened his mouth then closed it quickly. There was something going on here he hadn't got a handle on. If he intended to stick around Storm Creek for a while it might be smart to find out more. And he had a notion Mackay would tell him. Instead of the loud protest he'd been about to make, he nodded.

'Sure, Mr Mackay. Coffee would be fine.'

He waited until Mackay came down to the street and then climbed to the boardwalk and pushed open the door to the sheriff's office. The interior was the usual set-up. A scarred wooden desk stood over to his left, a wooden chair with arm rests behind it. In front of the desk two armless chairs stood alongside each other. The planked floor was covered with a dark rug of some material showing burn holes. In the centre of the back wall there was a solid door which probably led to the cages at the rear of the building. To the right of the door a stout wooden cabinet was pinned to the wall. Stafford guessed it held long guns.

Over to his right a blackened stove stood a couple of feet in front of the whitewashed wall, the stove pipe reaching to push through a hole in the stucco roof. Steam rose above the stove from the spout of a metal pot. He crossed the office, took down a tin cup and poured thick black coffee from the pot. In front of the desk he nudged the two chairs apart and sat down on one, placing the coffee on the desk.

He was maybe halfway down his coffee when Mackay came through the door. Stafford watched him silently as the sheriff went across to the stove to pour his own coffee before taking his place behind the desk. Mackay opened a drawer and took out two cheap cigars, handing one across to Stafford who pulled out a match from his vest pocket and lit them both.

'OK, Mr Stafford, tell me what went on back there.'

For a moment Stafford remained silent. He'd been smart to keep his mouth shut ten minutes earlier. But Mackay was sure turning out to be full of surprises.

'I was on the western trail an' I heard a shot,' he began.

As if making an army report he described the events from the time he'd heard the shot to when he'd delivered Brand to Mackay. When he'd finished, Mackay puffed a couple of times on his cigar, and then nodded.

'Yeah, reckoned it mighta been somethin' like that.'

'Then why the hell didn't you do somethin' about it?'

'Take it easy, Mr Stafford,' Mackay said. He pointed towards the window. 'What d'you see out there?'

Stafford shrugged. 'A prosperous little town.'

Mackay nodded. 'An' it's like that 'cos it's quiet.' He puffed at his cigar. 'An' I aim to keep it that way. Ten years ago it was a tougher town than Abilene. Then I came back from the War an' pinned on the badge. Now we got peace an' folks in town can go about their business.'

He held up a hand as Stafford began to speak.

'Sure, we had a killin' last week, but I got the killer back in the cage, an' the town's quiet agin.'

'That's a real fancy history lesson, Sheriff,' Stafford said. 'But what's this got to do with me and Brand?'

Mackay looked at him thoughtfully. 'How long you gonna be 'round these parts?'

Stafford shrugged. 'A month maybe. No more. I gotta get back to work.'

'Then you'd better know what goes on hereabouts. Frank Brand's the only son of Elias Brand who owns the Double B. Elias owns this town. Sure, he don't have paper on every ribbon clerk in Storm but without the ranch, or the men who work for him, or the stores he ships through the town, or anythin' else he buys and sells, most folks 'round here would be flat-busted inside o' six months.'

Stafford had one rule when playing poker: know when you're beat. Forget the whole damn business, he decided. If the crazy young fool hadn't taken a shot at him, he'd have probably kicked his butt and made him walk into town. It seemed that Elias Brand not only owned every ribbon clerk in town, he also owned Mackay. The sheriff addressing Brand as 'Mr Frank' told Stafford all he needed to know. Maybe his thoughts showed on his face for Mackay shook his head.

'I ain't for sale, if that's what you're thinkin'. I'm just bein' smart. I get Miss Morris up from South Pass to try the case...' He broke off and waved a hand in the air, seeing Stafford's change of expression. 'You're in Wyoming Territory now, Mr Stafford. We got ladies doing all sort of jobs since '69. We've even given 'em the vote.' Mackay leaned forward and crushed out the stub of his cigar.

26

'Anyways, say we got into court. It's gonna be your word against young Brand's. Who's Miss Morris gonna believe? The only son of the biggest ranch 'round these parts or some stranger who's just ridden into town?'

Stafford stubbed out his own cigar and got to his feet. 'You've made your case, Mr Mackay. I'll be about my business.'

Mackay looked up at him. 'You ain't tol' me yet why you're here.'

Stafford couldn't help grinning. Mackay was a real piece of work, he decided. 'Nothin' for you to worry about, Sheriff. Just visitin' an old friend.'

'Who–?' Mackay broke off, as the door from the boardwalk opened, and a young man just old enough to be out of breeches pushed his head into the office.

'Stagecoach comin' in, Sheriff,' he announced.

Mackay got to his feet. 'Thanks, Tommy, I'll be straight over.' He picked up a bunch of keys from his desk. 'I'll see you around, Mr Stafford. Buy you a whiskey in the Nugget.'

Stafford nodded. 'Reckon I'll take a beer 'cross there now.'

Five minutes after settling his two horses with the livery-man he was pushing through the batwing doors of the Nugget saloon. At this hour of the day the place was quiet. A bunch of cowboys sat around a table, cards and jugs of beer in front of them. Over to Stafford's left a solitary figure stood at the long bar which stretched the whole length of the long wall. Beyond the group of tables occupied by the cowboys a raised platform jutted from the rear wall. As fancy a place as in Dodge, Stafford decided. But a darn sight quieter. He walked to the bar as the saloon keeper he'd seen earlier that day moved along the bar to greet him.

'Howdy, stranger. Welcome to Storm.'

Stafford nodded. 'I'll take a beer.'

Something moved at the edge of his vision and he shifted to see the solitary drinker moving along the bar towards him. Some townsman, he decided, wanting to hear what had happened between him and Brand.

'Here y'are, George. I'll get that.'

Stafford sized up the speaker. He was maybe the same age as himself, late thirties, wearing what looked like the pants of a city suit, no jacket, a fancy silk vest over a plain blue shirt buttoned to the neck.

'You always buy beers for a stranger?' Stafford asked.

The man smiled showing large even teeth.

'Maybe we can do business,' he said. He took a small card from the fob pocket of his vest and placed it on the bar alongside the glass of beer put there by George.

Stafford glanced down. 'Henry J. Galton Photographer' the card read, and Stafford smiled, remembering the anxious little man in a town back on the trail. Taking a photograph in the town's Main Street, he'd used too much powder and covered the family group with black soot.

'Think on it, sir. You'll be recorded for history.' Galton exclaimed. 'A hundred years hence folks will look at my work and your great-grandchildren will tell with wonder of your adventures in the West.'

Stafford threw back his head and let out a roar of laughter. 'Mr Galton, I aim to stay out of adventures an' that includes gettin' hogtied by a lady. But I'll keep this while I'm in town.' He picked up the card and slipped it into the pocket of his trail jacket.

'Give Mr Galton a beer on me, George. The name's Luke Stafford,' he said to Galton, holding out his hand. Galton shook his hand with a stronger grip than Stafford expected.

'Most folks call me Harry,' Galton said. 'An' always ready to make a picture for you.'

'Yeah, an' too ready to make pictures of those damn sod busters,' came a shout.

Stafford turned to see one of the cowboys getting up from the table, and he guessed he'd been the one to shout across the saloon. The cowboy, his gait a little unsteady, stepped towards them. Behind him the half-a-dozen cowboys, wearing big grins on their faces, were obviously waiting to see what was going to happen.

'Take it easy, Fred,' called George from behind the bar.

The cowboy called Fred reached a spot a couple of feet away from Galton and Stafford. 'I ain't talkin' to you, George, I'm talkin' to this fancy feller from 'Frisco.' He stepped closer to Galton and thrust his head forward, the redness of his eyes showing the beer he'd drunk that morning.

'You makin' pictures of those damn homesteaders. It ain't right! This is cow country. You oughta be takin' pictures out at the ranch. You just make them dirt farmers think they got a right to be here.' Fred's voice rose to a shout. 'Why you doin' that? You just tell me!'

'Because they pay me, Fred,' Galton said evenly. 'An' you cowboys don't. Remember?'

'You callin' us four-flushers?'

Fred shifted his feet. His shoulder dropped and his bunched fist swung towards Galton's face. Stafford wasn't sure what happened next. Galton appeared to half-turn, his right hand moving fast to clasp Fred's upper arm. Then he spun on his heel, his broad shoulders bringing Fred's weight with him. An instant later the cowboy was hurtling across the saloon to crash into the group of his companions. Cards and bottles flew from the table into the sawdust as the cowboys jumped to their feet, ducking away from flying glass, and swearing loudly. Fred rolled on his back, struggling to his knees.

'You goddamn pilgrim!'

His hand dropped to the scarred butt of his sidearm. Then he froze, his fingers stiff, staring across the saloon. Stafford stood side on, his arm extended, his Colt rock-still in his fist, aiming directly at the cowboy.

'Don't make a mistake, Fred,' he said softly. 'A saloon's a lousy place to die.' His eyes flickered towards the group of cowboys who stood by the table. 'Any o' you reach for your hip an' you'd better know what you're doin'.'

'We ain't got trouble with you, stranger,' one of the cowboys called out.

'No, you ain't,' Stafford replied. 'But you're gonna settle your bill with George an'

31

walk outa here. Me an' Mr Galton are gonna finish our beers in peace.'

He lowered his Colt to hold it loosely by his side. 'Any o' you fellers got a notion to wait in the street an' you're gonna die there. You should know I do this for a livin'.'

Five minutes later Stafford and Galton were alone at the bar, save for a couple of storekeepers who'd dropped by for a noon-time drink. George had bought them both another beer, apologizing for their being troubled.

Stafford took the top off his beer. 'That was a fancy business you showed the cow-boy,' he said to Galton. 'I coulda used some-thin' like that a few times.'

'Coupla old men in San Francisco showed me how. Both musta been sixty years old. They kicked me 'round for a coupla years 'til I got smart. I'll tell you about it some-time.' Galton drew on his roll-up and blew smoke above the bar. 'You gonna be 'round these parts for long?'

Stafford shook his head. 'Just visitin' a friend. You can tell me where I'll find him. His name's Worley.'

Galton was suddenly still. 'Tom Worley? The lawyer feller?'

'That's him.'

Galton breathed in deeply. 'Tom Worley's in Sheriff Mackay's jail. They say he murdered a girl coupla days ago.'

CHAPTER THREE

After Mackay had shut the heavy door behind him, Stafford stood for a few seconds in the short passageway allowing his vision to adjust to the dim light. The floor of the passageway was hardpacked dirt, the wall showed rough unplaned timber. There were two cells, an afterthought Stafford realized, added to the rear of building when it had become the sheriff's office. To his left, vertical iron bars from roof to ground spanning the width of the cells gave a clear view of their interiors.

The first cell was empty. The man who sat on the bunk in the end cell remained intent on the papers in his hand. He was tall and slim, with a thick shock of black hair above pale, even features. Without looking up, he spoke.

'I'll need more books, Mr Mackay. I've money at the bank for them.'

Stafford remained silent, looking at his friend. For a man about to stand trial and maybe heading for the gallows Worley seemed remarkably steady.

'Tom Worley. How the hell d'you get into this barrel o' tar?'

Worley looked up sharply. For a moment his face was marked with a puzzled frown which then cleared to show a beaming smile. He threw down the paper among several others on his bunk and leapt to his feet, stepping towards the bars to grab Stafford's right hand in his own.

'Luke! Luke Stafford! God, I'm glad to see you. What the blazes brought you here?'

Stafford reached his free hand through the bars to grasp Worley by the shoulder as he clasped his friend's hand. 'I was south o' here in Truckee, an' remembered your letter sayin' you'd left Boston to come out West. Seemed a good chance to come an' drink your whiskey.' But then his expression became sombre. 'Didn't expect to find you like this.'

Worley took a pace back, turning away from Stafford. As if repeating an exercise he'd carried out a thousand times he paced to the wall, turned and returned to the bars. He rubbed his hand across his mouth as if trying to decide what he should say next. Then he thrust a hand through the bars and pointed along the passage.

'There should be a chair at the end,' he said.

Stafford brought the chair in front of the bars as Worley pulled forward the small stool which had stood by his bunk. The men sat a couple of feet apart separated by the cold, iron bars.

'I didn't kill her, Luke! You have to believe me, for what's damn sure only a couple of people in this town will.'

Stafford held up a hand. Maybe he'd been mistaken thinking his old friend was steady. Worley's face, now he'd recovered from his surprise, was marked with stress. Dark shadows showed beneath his eyes, fine lines showed at the corner of his mouth.

'Take it easy, Tom,' Stafford said. 'I only got into town a couple of hours ago. If I'm gonna help, I need to know everything. Start at the beginning.'

Worley took a deep breath. 'There's a lady hereabouts I wish to marry.' He looked sharply at Stafford. 'I know what you're thinking, Luke, but this time I mean it.' His mouth pulled up. 'But there is a problem.'

Stafford bit back the remark he was tempted to make. The time they'd spent together in the army had been marked with the dalliances of the handsome Worley with a

36

variety of pretty girls. He remembered a particular occasion at Fort Baxter. The daughter of the colonel commanding the fort had been locked in her room to prevent her seeing Worley. On more than one occasion his friend had only been saved from irate fathers and brothers by their regiment moving on. Stafford grunted with impatience. He was willing to wager that more than one woman was involved in this damned jackpot.

'She married already?' he asked.

Worley shook his head vehemently. 'No! I swear she has no husband. But take my word we've good reasons to be discreet. We've been meeting secretly at the Majestic.' He looked hard at Stafford. 'She's nothin' to do with my being in this place, an' I want her kept out of it. I'm not going to tell you her name, Luke, so don't ask.'

Stafford nodded. If it mattered he'd find out soon enough. 'So, who's the dead woman?'

'Not a woman, just a young girl. Lucy Andrews, daughter of Josh Andrews who owns the general store.' Worley bit hard on his lip, thinking. 'I got this note askin' me to go to the Majestic. I thought it was from...' He broke off for a moment. 'Anyways, I went to the room in the hotel that was mentioned in the note.'

Worley's head sank to his chest and stayed there for a few seconds before he again looked up at Stafford. 'The body of Lucy Andrews was on the floor. Her skirts were torn, her shirt ripped from her body. Her throat had been cut. The knife was by her side.' Worley shook his head as if trying to remove the scene from his mind's eye. 'Luke, I don't know to this moment why the hell I didn't call out for someone. But I saw that it was my knife with all that blood!'

'What did you do?'

'I grabbed the knife and ran from the room, straight into a couple of town councilmen coming up the stairs.'

Stafford frowned. 'Now hold on. Coupla minutes ago Mackay told me you've been a respected lawyer in this town. Who's gonna believe you were tied in with some young gal from a general store?'

Worley avoided Stafford's gaze. 'That's the trouble, Luke. I was.'

Stafford's hand shot through the bars to grasp Worley roughly by the arm. 'For Chris'sakes, Tom! D'you never learn? An' you talkin' sweet about gettin' married an' all.'

'No, Luke! You got the wrong idea,' Worley

protested. 'Sure, Lucy could be a trifle forward for such a young girl, but you have to believe me.' His hand gripped one of the bars. 'I swear it, Luke! Lucy Andrews was only a friend, an' I didn't kill her. My knife disappeared the night my clapboard got burned down. I've been set up, Luke, and I can guess who's behind it.'

Worley had half risen from his stool, his voice louder, his words tumbling over each other. As Stafford remained silent, his eyes hard, Worley slumped back, his head down, as if exhausted by his appeals to his friend.

'You don't believe what I'm saying,' he said bitterly.

'I didn't say that,' Stafford said harshly. 'You sayin' some critter's out to destroy you. Why would anyone have a mind to do that?'

Worley raised his head. 'I've been speaking for the few homesteaders that are left. Elisha Brand out at the Double B is hell bent on all the homesteaders packin' their wagons an' moving on. He's hired men to drive them off. Plenty of families have given in and headed further west. A few are still holding out, an' I was beginning to win my case for them, but Brand's a ruthless son of a bitch. He thinks the open range belongs to him. He sees me as an enemy. He's behind all this, I'm damn sure of it.'

Stafford frowned. Maybe his friend was no longer thinking straight.

'Are you sayin' that a powerful rancher went into the Majestic and cut this gal's throat?'

Worley shook his head furiously. 'No! I ain't saying that at all. But he's got men out there who'd do it if he gave the orders and paid enough.'

'It don't help none,' Stafford rapped out, 'but it don't seem you've been very smart takin' him on. I've heard Brand runs things 'round these parts. Why you worryin' 'bout a few dirt farmers?'

Worley looked his friend straight in the eye. 'The homesteaders who've stuck it out are all men from our old regiment. I reckon I owe it to them. Maybe you do, too.'

For a few moments Stafford sat quite still, silently digesting this latest information. The men in the regiment had been fine soldiers but there was no question of his taking Worley's place. Dragget's Wood would still be strong in their minds.

He looked directly at Worley. This man who could be heading for the gallows was the same man who'd carried him two and half miles at Ream's Station. Formal battle lines had been abandoned and they'd been separated from their men, pinned down for a while by Johnny Reb riflemen. He, Stafford, had been hit by a minie. With both their horses shot from beneath them, their only option was to head back to their own lines on foot. Stafford had managed 500 yards before collapsing. Tom Worley had got him to the surgeons in time.

'How long you got before the trial?'

Worley shrugged. 'Mackay doesn't know.'

'You ain't finished yet, Tom.'

He thrust his hand through the bars and clasped Worley's hand. As Stafford got to his feet Worley picked up a book from his bunk.

'I need to get that back to Mrs Victoria Ross at the schoolroom,' he said, handing the book through the bars.

Stafford, carrying the book he was returning for Worley, was ten feet from the door of the schoolhouse when he heard the sweet notes of a fine piano. He stopped still on the path, surprised by the unexpected sound. The only schoolhouse he'd been into out west had barely enough McGuffey's *Readers* for each child. The notion of finding a piano in such a place was as likely as finding an elephant from the continent of Africa. Storm Creek, he decided, was a place full of surprises. He reached the door, pausing for a few moments as he listened to the gentle notes. Then he tapped on the door, and pushed it open. The music stopped suddenly.

Lines of wooden tables, their tops lit by the early afternoon sun that shone through the small windows over to Stafford's right, filled maybe half of the room. Beyond a larger table standing towards the rear of the room sat a woman in the shadows before a high-backed piano. On the floor beside her, on tensed legs, stood a black and white dog, its tongue lolling, its head turned in Stafford's direction. From the animal's throat came a low growl. The woman put a hand on the dog's head.

'Stay!' she ordered.

Stafford pulled off his battered Stetson and edged his way through the desks towards her.

'The name's Stafford, ma'am. I'm a friend of Tom Worley.' He glanced at the animal. 'That's a sheepman's dog, ain't it?'

The woman got up from her stool and stepped away from the shadows, rearranging her blue woollen skirt. She moved towards the centre of the room. As she did so the rays of sunlight lit up her face and her long slender neck. Her fair hair was piled on the top of her head and her blue eyes gazed directly at Stafford.

'A Scottish border collie,' she said, answering his question. 'One of the homesteaders left him behind when they packed up and left. They called him Ruffian, but I think Ruff suits him better.' She smiled, showing even teeth. 'You must be Tom's friend from the army.'

'Word travels fast in this town,' Stafford said. He held up the book he was carrying. 'From Tom,' he said. 'I'm sorry I broke up your playin'. I didn't expect to hear the music of Chopin in Storm Creek.'

The woman lifted fine eyebrows as she glanced at the sidearm on his hip. 'Are you a musician, Mr Stafford?'

Stafford shook his head. 'My mother taught music in the old country. She gave me lessons until I was ten.' He grinned. 'I guess she gave up on me after that. You must be Mrs Victoria Ross,' he added.

She nodded and the smile on her face faded. 'How is Mr Worley?'

'He's well, but Mackay told me he'll be in jail some time. For a murder trial a judge has to come up from Cheyenne, an' that's gonna take a while.'

43

Victoria Ross blinked rapidly. 'Poor Tom. I can't bear the thought of what might happen to him.'

'You think he killed Lucy Andrews?'

She shook her head vehemently. 'Of course not. But everything seems so against him. Tom and Lucy were only friends. He was trying to help her.'

Stafford breathed in deeply. He knew that if Worley hadn't given his word he might find it difficult to believe what Victoria Ross had just said.

'Lucy Andrews was too forward,' she continued. 'I knew her well. She helped with the children here for a while. As with all young girls she had her dreams. She talked of being taken to a big city, Chicago, San Francisco, anywhere, if it took her away from Storm Creek.'

She looked towards the windows. 'Two years ago she scandalized the town. Lucy did not behave as a young lady should.' She looked back at Stafford. 'We're a small town, Mr Stafford. The young men here have small town habits. When Tom arrived in town with his city manners and style she was totally smitten.'

'And what did Tom think of all this?'

'He treated her like a young sister, always

44

trying to persuade her that she could be happy in Storm. He encouraged her to be more modest and demure. She used to fight against his counsel, demanding more of him than he was prepared to give.' She shook her head regretfully. 'Of late she'd be as sweet as molasses one day, then act badly the next. The day before she was killed, she and Tom had a falling out. They must have exchanged words in the store, but their arguing spilled outside. Half the town heard their angry voices.'

Stafford bit his lip with exasperation. The more he heard the worse became Worley's chances of avoiding the hangman. On what he'd learned so far a jury would convict without leaving the box. But Worley had given him his word. That was good enough for him. He wasn't about to abandon his old friend in time of desperate need. He became aware that Victoria Ross was gazing at him intently with her deep-blue eyes.

'I really didn't think you were a musician, Mr Stafford.' The tip of her tongue touched her upper lip. 'Are you here to help Tom?'

Stafford nodded. He put the book down on a nearby table. 'I'm gonna get Tom outa that jail. All legal, I hope. But I'll bust him out if I have to.'

Stafford stepped out along the boardwalk, his plains spurs jingling, as he headed for the two-storey building Worley had moved into after losing his clapboard. In his pocket was a list bearing the titles of books the lawyer needed from the bookshelf behind his desk.

Stafford was only vaguely aware of the sidelong glances of the townsfolk. He was turning over in his mind the conversation he'd had a few minutes before with Mackay. The sheriff had been as ornery as a mule. Sure, Mackay had said angrily, he knew Elias Brand was forcing out the homesteaders. What was he supposed to do? The homesteads were beyond the thirty-two square miles of his jurisdiction. The hard truth might stick in a man's gullet but out on the old open range the gun was law. Sure, times were changing but it was going to be some years before the rule of civilized law covered all the territory. Take on Brand's gunmen out there as an ordinary citizen and he'd be heading for Boot Hill. He was too close to retiring to his porch to be a hero.

Mackay must have reckoned he had a winning card. He'd heard that morning that

46

Stafford had been one of the homesteaders' officers. If Stafford was so tough maybe he should be doing something about Brand's gunmen. The two men had squared up to each other across the office like two prize-fighters meeting a day before their fight. Mackay wasn't about to budge an inch, and Stafford had stamped out of the office, his face taut with frustration.

Now, Stafford passed a painted sign nailed to the door of Harry Galton's store. In large red letters it announced that Galton had worked with the famous photographer of the War, Mr Mathew Brady. Stafford couldn't resist a grin, wondering if it was true or merely another ruse of Galton's to drum up business.

Twenty yards on he reached the board that announced Tom Worley's office. He turned off the boardwalk and mounted the steps that ran outside the building to the upper storey. Worley had told him to expect the outside door to his office to be unlocked. Sure enough, he turned the handle and stepped inside.

He had a brief impression of a large desk in front of a whitewashed wall and a large map when something hard hit him on the side of his head. His mind clouded, and his knees buckled. As he pitched forward, his hat flying ahead of him, he was kicked in both sides of his body. A clenched fist slammed down on the nape of his neck. He hit the floor, face first, bile surging into his mouth and spewing onto the floor. He pushed his hands hard against the wooden floor, attempting to lever himself onto his knees but sharp-toed boots hacked at his wrists. His face hit the floor again.

A hand grabbed his hair, hauling his head back. Through the black swirling clouds, shot through with red flashes of light, Stafford had a vague picture of a long, white, expressionless face without lips or nose from which stared black narrow eyes.

'You get this one warnin', Stafford! Quit Storm, or the next time we'll put you on Boot Hill!'

His head was smashed down onto the floor. The black clouds bloomed and filled his mind.

CHAPTER FOUR

Stafford opened his eyes. He was vaguely aware of a small square of harsh light somewhere above him. Closer, swirls of black and white swam before him. He blinked rapidly, attempting to bring his surroundings into focus. For one terrible moment he thought he was blind.

The pain in his chest was matched with the stab in his gut. Had a Johnny Reb sniper taken him out? Would he be able to ride? His mind raced, almost out of control. Worley was back with the colonel, there'd be nobody to carry him if he couldn't walk. His head began to clear and the swirls of black and white began to slow. After a few seconds he could read the map. Black lines marked the positions of the Johnny Rebs. Why had their officers spread them out so widely? It had to be dumbest tactical move he'd seen since the War started. The Rebs would be cut to pieces by the cavalry when the charge was ordered.

'Luke! Luke! You OK?'

That was Worley's voice. But he was positive that Tom was back with the colonel for the day. Again the shout came. How could it be so close?

'Luke! You hear me?'

Stafford shook his head, again blinking rapidly. His vision cleared, and the Johnny Reb lines turned into the cracks of the stucco wall a foot from his face. He raised his head, a searing pain cutting behind his eyes. Where the hell was he?

He pushed himself off the bunk, and slowly stood up. The iron bars of the cell caught the morning sun as it shone through the small window set high in the stucco wall. Christ! He was in the cell next to Worley.

'Tom!' Stafford called.

'Here, Luke. You OK?' There was a relieved note in Worley's voice.

'I feel like hell,' Stafford called.

He looked around at the mean little cell, a duplicate of the one Worley was occupying. Then he realized the door to his cell was open, and he took the couple of paces to take him out of the cell into the passageway. Worley was standing at the bars of his cell.

'What the hell went on, Luke? Mackay'll not tell me anything.'

'I got bushwhacked in your office. Mebbe four of 'em jumped me. Don't know what

50

the hell I'm doing here.' Stafford swallowed quickly, tasting the bile that came to the back of his throat. He put a hand to his forehead as pain stabbed behind his eyes once more.

'I reckon they were after these,' Worley said, pointing to the papers strewn across his bunk. 'Maybe Brand thinks I'll turn them over to another lawyer.' He pushed out a hand between the bars to steady Stafford who had shifted his feet to clutch at a bar.

'Doc Mayerling's a good man, Luke. You'd best see him.'

Stafford shook his head and instantly regretted it as sparks of light danced before his eyes. 'Mebbe tomorrow if I don't feel finer.' He screwed up his eyes until he was able to focus on the papers scattered across Worley's bunk. 'I recall seein' a big map in your place. You got anythin' like it, showing the homesteads an' with a proper scale?'

'Sure, much smaller than the one in my office, but it's the same.'

Worley turned to the bunk and scrabbled around until he found what he was looking for. He handed the map through the bars to Stafford who examined it carefully. Holding the map in one hand, he used the first and little fingers of his other hand as a rough

51

measuring instrument. He placed them on the scale then shifted them to make an estimate of distance. He nodded, satisfied.

'If the men'll listen to me, I think mebbe there's a way to make their life easier.' He looked directly at his friend. 'Any chance Joe Bagley's one of 'em?'

Worley nodded. 'I'll show you Bagley's place,' he said. He reached through the bars and took back the map from Stafford. He turned it around so Stafford could see the lines representing the 160 acres of Bagley's homestead.

'Probably forty miles from town. You get some rest, an' you'll make it easy tomorrow.'

'Sure,' Stafford said, taking back the map. And another day less before your trial, he thought. 'Stay steady, Tom. I'll be back.'

Worley's frown deepened. 'Remember what I said about Doc Mayerling.'

With a raised hand of acknowledgement Stafford moved down the passageway to open the door and step into the sheriff's office. Mackay sat behind the desk. He grunted with surprise.

'I guess you're even tougher than you look,' he said. 'I had you on that cell bunk for a coupla days.' He waved a hand. 'Get yourself some coffee.'

Stafford filled a cup from the pot, and took a large gulp of the hot black liquid. He could almost feel the blood in his veins quicken as the coffee streamed down to his gut.

'You gonna tell me how I got here?'

'Bunch of ex-soldiers from the homesteads hadn't heard about Worley an' that gal, an' came chasin' their lawyer. They walked into you gettin' stomped an' scared off the no-goods. Then they dumped you on the board-walk outside and tol' me what they'd found.'

Stafford took another sip of his coffee, slower this time. 'They say anythin' else?'

'Yeah, they weren't gonna see any man killed, but you could look after your own goddamned hide.'

Stafford nodded, as if unsurprised by Mackay's words. 'I'll go see 'em,' he said. He jerked a thumb towards the door leading to the cells.

'This trouble 'cross at Worley's office don't give you doubts about what's goin' on in this town?'

Mackay's face tautened. 'Now you just hold it there, Mr Stafford. I ain't sayin' Worley's guilty or innocent. I see a man runnin' from a killin' carryin' the knife that cut a gal's throat then I'm gonna put him in jail. A judge an' jury's gonna decide if he's

53

guilty or not.'

Stafford's mouth twitched. 'I guess I was out o' order there, Mr Mackay.' He stood up, and for a second the figure of Mackay seemed to swing away from him before swinging back again in focus.

'You better take it easy.' Mackay's voice sounded to Stafford as if it was coming out of an ear trumpet. 'Maybe you ain't as tough as you think.'

The light was beginning to fade as Stafford turned the palomino's head away from the rough track and urged the animal towards the two wooden cabins built on the side of sloping ground. He guessed that one was Bagley's home, the other some sort of barn for the animals.

He could make out a figure maybe fifty yards from the cabin over to his right walking steadily behind a simple plough drawn by a single horse. As Stafford closed the distance to the cabin, the plough was suddenly brought to a halt by the man hauling abruptly on the reins. Stafford saw him bend and straighten, turning in Stafford's direction. In his hands he now held a long gun.

'You ain't welcome, stranger,' the man called, raising the long gun to his shoulder.

'Don't come any closer. I'm givin' fair warnin'!'

Stafford reined in his mount to a walk, and continued to ride forward.

'Sergeant Bagley. Sergeant Joe Bagley?' he called out.

'Who in tarnation—?' The rifle came down from the man's shoulder.

'Cap'n Stafford? Cap'n Luke Stafford?' Amazement was written across Bagley's craggy face. 'Well, I'll be damned!'

Stafford reached Bagley, and swung his leg over the saddle of the palomino, the ache in his joints growing stronger as he stepped down to the ground, causing him to grimace with pain. He was aware of Bagley's enquiring gaze as they shook hands.

'I s'pose you come to Storm to visit the lieutenant,' Bagley said. 'Mighty good o' you to come out here, Cap'n. Mrs Bagley puts fine grub on the table, an' we can find you a bunk.' He looked down at the long gun, now resting by its stock on the ground. 'Don't pay no attention to this.' His shoulders lifted in resignation. 'I guess you've heard we got our troubles. Mr Worley's doin' great work for us, but that sonovabitch Brand an' his men are a pack of rascals.'

He turned towards the plough and picked

up the reins of the big grey that stood as still as a statue in the failing light. 'We'll just get ol' Molly her supper, an' you come an' meet the family.' He looked up proudly at Stafford. 'Got a coupla boys now, Cap'n.'

Something was wrong, Stafford realized. Bagley was talking as if nothing had changed in the last few days. He seemed unaware that Worley was in jail, or that some of the other ex-soldiers had saved his own hide before dumping him on the sheriff.

'Joe, when did you last meet with the other men?'

Stafford moved the palomino as Bagley turned the grey towards the barn that was just visible in the dusk. Bagley shrugged.

'Ten days maybe. We're all too busy this time o' the year for a lot of socializin'. I know that some o' the men were goin' into Storm yesterday to ask Mr Worley some questions.'

'Joe, I got some bad news–' Stafford stopped suddenly. The dusk of the evening had suddenly deepened to velvet black. That was mighty strange. The stars, too, had changed colour from sparkling silver to blood red. Did they do that hereabouts? He'd never seen that happen in Colorado. And why was Bagley first shouting at him and then whispering? He'd have to tell him he needn't call him captain any more. The War was over, or maybe he was just hoping for that and getting confused? Then his fingers slipped from the reins of his palomino and he pitched headfirst to the grass.

'Glad to have you back with us, Mr Stafford,' Bessy Bagley said.

Stafford looked at the semicircle of smiling faces around Joe Bagley's table. He put down his fork and leaned back. 'Joe's a lucky man to be married to such a fine cook,' he said. 'An' it's good to be eatin' real food again.' He looked at Bagley. 'How long I been out, Joe?'

'Coupla days, Cap'n.' Seeing Stafford's change of expression he added quickly, 'We sent a message into town. Mr Worley knows you're with us.'

Stafford nodded. 'I'm sure grateful to you all.'

'Daisy Morgan came over each day,' Bessy Bagley said. 'She'd done some nursin' in the War.'

'Then she did a great job,' said Stafford, and meant it. Despite the beating he'd taken he felt surprisingly well, almost light-headed. 'Joe, the blade on that plough o' yourn needs replacin'. I'll get one shipped from town.'

'Now, Cap'n, we ain't–' Bagley started to protest.

Stafford held up his hand. 'It'll be here in a few days,' he said. 'No more mention of it. We got more important business to talk about.'

'Then we'll be about our chores,' Bessy Bagley said. She got to her feet and addressed the two boys. 'C'mon now, there's lots to do.'

Stafford and Bagley got to their feet until the three had left them, staying silent until the door to the outside had closed. Back in their seats Stafford pulled from beneath his shirt the map that Worley had given him.

'I gotta real strong notion that the murder o' that gal and your troubles with Brand are connected. Mr Worley in jail is just too handy for Brand.' Seeing Bagley's expression, Stafford shook his head. 'No, don't ask me how. I gotta hunch, that's all.'

He placed the map on the table between them. 'I'm aimin' to get Mr Worley outa jail. But first, we stop Brand's men. Those no-goods drivin' folks away ain't cowboys, that's for sure. Brand must have hired gunslingers. I think I gotta plan to stop 'em.'

Bagley nodded. 'I think it's a good plan, Cap'n.'

Stafford, who'd been studying the map, looked up sharply. 'I ain't tol' you what it is yet.'

Bagley grinned. 'You've tol' me a dozen times this last coupla days; ravin' 'bout it just like we was gonna take on Johnny Reb years back. An' you were thinkin' Mr Worley was with you, tellin' him as well!'

Stafford's mouth twisted. If McParlen back in Boston had heard Bagley's words he might get to wondering if Stafford was slowing down. Maybe he was getting too old to be going up against a bunch of gunslingers taking their orders, and most likely plenty of money, from a powerful rancher. He pushed away the thought. His task was to get Tom Worley out of jail.

He looked directly at Bagley. 'You think the homesteaders will listen to me? I ain't a captain any more, Joe. Some of 'em, I hear, are men from the regiment. Mebbe they're still rememberin' Dragget's Wood.'

Bagley's face was expressionless. 'Come outside, Cap'n, an' we'll find out.' He stood up from the table and walked to the door where he stopped and looked back at Stafford who was staring back at him with a puzzled look on his weather-beaten face.

'All the homesteaders are waitin' for you,

Cap'n, an' they're all from the regiment. We're the only ones left.'

Stafford got to his feet. How had he got the notion that only a few of the homesteaders were ex-soldiers? Maybe he'd misunderstood Worley. But it made sense. Brand's gunmen would have soon scared away pilgrims from back East unused to facing threats from armed men. Who could blame the pioneers for packing their wagons and moving further west in search of a more peaceful place to build their cabins and harness their ploughs?

But would his plan now work as he intended? To be successful the plan needed men willing to risk their lives. The War had been over for ten years. Would the men still follow him?

He stepped through the open door behind Bagley. Ten yards from the door a dozen men stood in a closely knitted group, some silent, with pipes in their mouths, others talking to each other in low tones. As Bagley and Stafford stepped away from the house the men turned as if one, and stared stolidly in their direction.

'You all know the cap'n,' Bagley called out. 'He's got somethin' to say you're gonna want to hear.'

The men remained silent, all staring

impassively in Stafford's direction.

'I got three things to say,' Stafford said, his eyes scanning the group. 'First, I ain't a captain no longer. Nobody's gotta listen, they don't want to. They can walk away now.'

One of the men muttered something to his comrades, and a low noise of agreement rippled through the group. Stafford waited, but none of the men made a move.

'Some o' you still think o' Dragget's Wood. I know that. But I want to thank you for what you did the other day in Storm.'

'More than you did for that poor bastard Carlson,' said one, his face hard below the blue woollen cap that half-covered a shock of fair hair.

Stafford paused. There! It was out in the open. His face remained expressionless but he cursed inwardly. Hell! Bagley meant well. Maybe had there been fewer ex-soldiers and more men unknown to him he'd have got a better hearing. If the murder of Lucy Andrews and these attacks on the homesteaders were connected, as he was convinced, should he turn his mind first to finding the girl's real killer?

Bagley stepped forward to face the group. 'The cap'n's gotta plan to stop those varmints raidin' us from the Double B,' Bagley said. 'You wanna hear it or not?'

A short, stocky man, wrapped in a red mackinaw spoke up from the back. 'Cap'n always had good plans,' he said. 'Remember that day at Stony Creek Depot? Johnny Reb woulda cut us to pieces without the cap'n's plan.'

There was a loud noise of agreement from the assembled men. 'Go ahead, Cap'n',' one of the men called out.

Stafford took a deep breath. He held up the map he was carrying. 'OK, gather 'round.' He looked around at the group. 'You all see this?' He paused a few moments while the men shuffled into a half circle, enabling everyone to see where Stafford was pointing on the map.

Slowly, making sure every man understood the sequence of events he had in mind, Stafford explained his plan. Several times he stopped to answer questions, and once, after a suggestion by Bagley, he changed a detail. Finally, having knelt to cut lines in the dirt to explain the final parts of the plan, Stafford stood up. He stared hard at the men.

'I ain't aimin' for a bloodbath, but lead's gonna be flyin'. Men are gonna get killed. We stand firm an' it ain't gonna be one of us.'

'But it could be,' said one of the men, Corporal Jenkins, Stafford remembered.

Stafford nodded. 'Any man here goes down I'll give his family enough money for a fresh start. Nobody's gonna be wantin'.'

There was a murmur of noise among the men.

'Why would you do that, Cap'n?' Jenkins said.

Stafford didn't answer the question directly. He rested his gaze on each of the ex-soldiers in turn before speaking.

'Any man here reckons Mr Worley killed that girl?'

The men stirred, exchanging angry looks. Loud voices were raised at the notion that their lieutenant from the War could be guilty of such a terrible act.

'An' that's my thinkin',' Stafford said. 'Together we're gonna stop Brand, an' I'll spend my last cent if it means we get Mr Worley outa that jail.'

The ex-soldier in the blue woollen cap who'd challenged Stafford over Dragget's Wood took his pipe from his mouth.

'Mebbe it's good you came along, Cap'n', he said.

CHAPTER FIVE

The hotel clerk in the Majestic was a man of about thirty with a scar over his right eyebrow. He wore a brown city suit, the jacket with its four buttons a little too tight over his deep chest. His black hair, already beginning to thin, was slicked down with oil.

'We have a most comfortable room overlooking Main Street, Mr Stafford,' he said. 'From it you will have an excellent view of the townsfolk as they go about their business.'

Stafford shook his head. 'I'll take the room above the alleyway.'

The clerk, whose name Stafford had learned was Kenney, looked uncomfortable. 'Mr Stafford, I have to tell you–'

Kenney hesitated, appearing to be torn between honesty and the chance to make money. Stafford guessed the room where Lucy Andrews had been killed would have been left vacant until memories faded.

'I know about the killing,' Stafford said. 'I'll still take the room.'

'Very well,' the clerk said quickly. He snatched at a large brass key as if nervous that Stafford would change his mind.

'I've boxes at the livery. Have someone bring 'em over.'

'At once, Mr Stafford.' His eyes dropped to the Navy Colt on Stafford's hip, and he bit his lip. 'I'm sorry but...' His voice trailed away.

Stafford's mouth twitched. 'Relax, Mr Kenney. You can hang it on a peg behind you when I come back later.' He looked at the clock above Kenney's head. 'You know a respectable boarding-house where a married lady alone would be comfortable?'

'Widow Brown's,' Kenney said promptly. 'The clapboard beyond the blacksmith.' Again he hesitated. 'She does gossip, though.'

Stafford remained expressionless. This was proving better than he'd hoped for. 'Much obliged, Mr Kenney.'

He glanced again at the clock, then turned on his heel and went out into Main Street. The townsfolk were about their business. A young woman in her twenties carrying a basket of eggs stole a glance at him from her lowered head as she passed. A few yards on, Stafford became aware that a tall man dressed in blue working clothes was glaring at him from the doorway of the general store. Josh Andrews, maybe? He didn't turn his head in the man's direction.

He walked past more stores until the boardwalk finished a few yards past the door of the bathhouse. He pulled forward one of the wooden chairs that were lined up on the boardwalk, leaned it on its back legs and sat with his feet up on the rail. In front of him the hardpack of Main Street gave way to the rougher ground of the trail into town. For the next ten minutes a steady stream of wagons and riders passed to and fro in front of him.

He took his feet off the rail and pushed back his chair when he saw the buckboard driven by Joe Bagley appear around the bend in the trail. He pinched out the roll-up he'd been smoking, and stepped down to the hardpack. Bagley hauled back on the reins and halted the buckboard alongside him.

'Mornin', Joe. Good day, Mrs Morgan.' Stafford flicked a finger to the brim of his hat.

'Seems my nursin' did the trick, Mr Stafford,' Daisy Morgan said.

Stafford grinned. 'Sure did, ma'am. I'm mighty grateful.' He turned to Bagley. 'The clapboard beyond the livery, Joe. Then you can be about your business.'

'OK, Cap'n.'

Bagley tapped the grey on its flanks and moved the buckboard forward slowly as Stafford stepped back up to the boardwalk, striding out to keep pace with Bagley and his passenger. Outside Widow Brown's clapboard Stafford stepped down to the street again to assist Daisy Morgan alight from the buckboard. Bagley took down her canvas bag and handed it to Stafford before climbing back into his seat. Exchanging farewells with Stafford, he urged the grey forward and continued down Main Street.

'Let's get you settled, Mrs Morgan,' Stafford said.

There was the sound of a door opening. He turned to find a buxom woman in black bombazine standing in the threshold of the clapboard. Her ample bosom and her wide black skirts seemed to fill the doorway. Grey curls of wispy hair peeped beneath the little white cap on her head.

'A guest for you, ma'am,' he said. 'Mrs Morgan's gonna stay for a few days while her husband's in Cheyenne.'

'A dollar a day, a dollar fifty with supper, Mrs Morgan,' Widow Brown said. 'I hope that's acceptable.'

'I'll be settling Mrs Morgan's account,' Stafford said. 'You'll find me at the Majestic. An' by the way, Mrs Morgan does like hot biscuits with her meals. If they're extra, I'll pay.'

He patted Daisy Morgan on her arm. 'You enjoy the rest, Mrs Morgan.'

Stafford picked up her bag to carry it into the house. He turned to the widow. 'Mrs Morgan's likely to be with you a while. I hear Mr Morgan'll be away several days.'

Ten minutes later Stafford reached the store occupied by Harry Galton. His mouth twitched as he again read Galton's claim to have worked with Mathew Brady. He stepped through the open door, wrinkling his nose as the smell of chemicals wafted through a rear door. Galton looked up from behind the table where he was adding figures in a book.

Stafford jerked his thumb behind him. 'You really work with Mathew Brady?'

Galton nodded, a serious look on his face. 'Sure, I did. All through his time in the War. My word on it.'

'Brady was with us at Petersburg,' Stafford said. 'Don't remember seein' you.'

For a second or two Galton remained silent. Then he put up a hand in mock

68

surrender, a grin creasing his face. 'When Mr Brady's sight began to fail I became his body-guard,' Galton said. 'The men who worked for him showed me what they were doin'.' His lips pulled back from his teeth. 'After the War was over I was mighty tired o' getting' shot at, so I set myself up in San Francisco making pictures afore I moved here.'

'Maybe I shoulda done something like that,' Stafford said, shrugging his shoulders. He turned away from Galton for a moment to look around the room. 'Tell me, Mr Galton, what stops you making good pictures?'

'Movement an' bad light,' Galton said promptly. 'Folks back East are workin' on it but they ain't found the answers yet.' He grinned. 'Mr Brady used to get real ornery when folks moved around.'

'OK, movement ain't gonna be a problem. We'll see about the light.'

Stafford took out coins from his vest pocket and laid them on the table in front of Galton. After asking a couple of questions and getting the answers he was hoping for, he spent a few minutes outlining what he wanted from Galton.

'What d'you reckon?' Stafford asked when he'd finished.

Galton frowned. 'I ain't promisin' but it's

69

worth tryin'. Gimme twenty minutes.'

'You got 'em. Maybe more.'

Stafford left Galton and continued his way along the boardwalk. He knew he was taking a gamble and he could be too late. Four days had gone by. What he had in mind would depend on the habits and customs of this small town. Some places he'd been, four days would have been three days too late. But maybe Storm Creek was different. He hoped so.

He halted outside the funeral parlour. Fancy black letters on glass announced the establishment of 'J. Smallwood, Undertaker'. Stafford pushed open the door. There was a variety of scents from the flowers that stood in pots around the room. A man sat behind a pinewood desk on which stood a brass inkstand and an old-fashioned stove-pipe hat.

The man stood up as Stafford stepped forward. He was round-shaped. A round head on a round body dressed in funereal black, lightened only by the white shirt beneath his black silk vest. His tongue moistened his lips before he spoke.

'I fervently hope this is not too sad a day for you,' he said in a low syrupy tone.

'Sit down, Smallwood,' Stafford said.

'We're gonna talk business.'

He pulled across the chair, placed it in front of the desk, and straddled it, his arms resting on the back of the chair.

'I don't think–' Smallwood began.

'That's right, Smallwood. Don't think too much, an' you might get to make some money.'

Smallwood sank back into his seat, the expression in his eyes changing from protest to greedy interest at Stafford's mention of money. Stafford reached into his pocket, and placed two coins on the desk. The sun, shining over his shoulder, lit up the silver.

Smallwood licked his lips again. 'And what is it you want?'

'You boxed up Lucy Andrews yet?'

Smallwood's Adam's apple bobbled in his throat. 'I don't think–'

Stafford reached across and pulled Smallwood towards him by the lapel of his black jacket. 'I tol' you once. Don't be doing any thinkin'.'

He released the lapel and Smallwood fell back in his chair, his face red, eyes darting between Stafford and the coins on the desk. His breathing was suddenly quick and jerky.

'No,' he said finally, his voice weak. 'She's gonna be boxed up today. Doc Mayerling is gonna do some stitchin' afore her family come on round.'

Stafford nodded, satisfied. 'I wanna see her.'

Smallwood's eyes opened wide. 'You cain't do that! I ain't sure what you're about, but you're that Stafford feller, ain't you? Mackay'd run me outa town I let you do that.'

With a hand as brown and hard as mahogany Stafford pushed the coins across the desk to Smallwood. A grim smile began to show on his face as mixed feelings flitted across the face of the undertaker. Smallwood pulled out a large spotted handkerchief from a slit pocket in his coat, and dabbed at the perspiration that had begun to show on his pale forehead. Slowly he stood up from the chair.

'If Mackay finds out, I'm finished,' he said weakly.

'Nobody's gonna know,' Stafford said.

Smallwood stepped from behind his desk and made his way to the door at the rear of the room closely followed by Stafford. He opened the door and the scent of pine came strongly to Stafford's nostrils. Over to the right, funeral caskets, some only half finished, rested on trestles of rough timber. His boots brushed against wood shavings littering the stone floor.

In the centre of the large room, maybe ten feet in front of large double doors stood a pine table maybe six and a half feet long. On it a long white sheet outlined the shape of a body.

'Turn the sheet back,' Stafford ordered, as he approached the table. 'I need to see her.'

Smallwood, who'd moved to the other side of the table in front of the double doors bent forward. Carefully he folded back the cloth until it showed the beginning of the swell of the dead girl's breasts.

'That's enough,' Stafford said.

Even in death, her even features showed that in life Lucy Andrews had been a very pretty girl. At her throat the cut that ended her life showed as two lines separating the open wound. No wonder Smallwood had called in the doctor to do what he could. No mother or father would wish to see their child like this.

But why was she killed? Worley believed Elias Brand had a hand in her death, throwing the blame on him in order to remove him. But maybe that was too simple. He'd been told twice that Lucy Andrews was too forward. Had she been having assignations with someone important in the town and threatened to tell? Or maybe she'd stumbled on something in the hotel room and had to be killed to keep her mouth shut?

He moved to one end of the table on which the body lay. 'Get the other end o' the table,' he ordered Smallwood. 'We're gonna move her closer to the doors.'

'What–'

Smallwood stopped suddenly, seeing Stafford's expression and moved to the end of the table, lifting it as ordered. When the table was close to the door Stafford stepped back and put a hand in his pocket. Then he leaned forward and placed a coin alongside the body within reach of Smallwood. The undertaker's eyes opened wide.

'That's a gold piece,' Stafford said. 'Minted in California, worth thirty-six dollars.'

Panic showed in Smallwood's eyes. 'We ain't doin' anything agin the laws o' the Good Lord!'

'All you gotta do is open them doors,' Stafford said, pointing. 'I'm tol' you got high walls 'round your yard. Nobody's gonna see from the street.'

Once more Smallwood wet his lip with the tip of his tongue. 'An' I get the gold piece?'

'You get the gold piece.'

Smallwood stepped across to the doors.

For a moment he wrestled with bolts before flinging open the doors allowing light to stream into the room. Smallwood let out a strangled cry.

'Omigod!' He spun around. 'You tol' me nobody would know!'

Six feet from the open door Galton stood alongside his photographic equipment. His big square camera resting on its tripod gave the appearance of a menacing animal from another world.

'Shut your mouth, Smallwood. You're part of this, now,' Stafford said harshly. He called out to Galton. 'Can you do it, Harry?'

'Reckon so, Luke.'

'Make sure you get the cuts on her throat,' Stafford said.

Kenney was still at his post in the Majestic when Stafford returned. He unbuckled his gunbelt and handed it across the counter. The clerk picked it up as if handling a rattler and hung it on one of the wooden pegs. Save for an old .31 Colt cap-lock with a scarred butt and dust on its barrel the other pegs were empty.

'Your boxes are in your room, Mr Stafford.' Kenney hesitated, as if searching for the right words. 'I hope you find everything to your liking.'

Stafford took the large brass key from the clerk. 'I hope so, Mr Kenney.'

He went up to the stairs to the right of Kenney's desk until he reached a shadowy corridor which ran to a window at the end overlooking the alleyway. His door was to the right of the window. He unlocked it, and for a moment stood at the threshold letting his gaze wander around the room.

Save for an obviously new rug in the middle of the room he saw nothing special. He must have been in a hundred similar rooms in the last ten years; a bed and chair, a small table, a mirror in a metal frame. Over to his right stood a credenza on which rested a white china pitcher and jug. Next to the credenza was a tall cupboard for clothes, its long door slightly ajar. His own boxes stood on the floor beneath a cheap mezzotint of some foreign landscape hanging on the wall opposite the window that overlooked the alleyway.

Stafford stepped into the room and closed the door behind him. He took off his hat and hung it on the wooden peg fixed to the door. After unbuckling his spurs he stepped forward and dropped to one knee to pull back the new rug. If he hadn't known about the killing he would have paid no attention

76

to the faint stain on the boards. He replaced the rug and again looked around the room.

'Let's see what we got here,' he said aloud.

Methodically he began to search the room. He placed the jug and its bowl on the bed while he moved the credenza. Behind it, all he found were dust balls. He took out the drawers of the credenza one by one, but they were empty. His fingers, running along the wood, told him there was nothing behind them.

'Guess I should have a woman here,' he said, again aloud, as he pulled apart the bed. Five minutes later he was laboriously replacing blankets. He searched the cupboard but its dark interior revealed nothing.

Maybe he was wasting his time. The hotel people would have made every effort to remove any trace of Lucy Andrews's killing. The new rug and the efforts to scrub out the bloodstains proved that. Yet they hadn't been as thorough as they might have been. The dust behind the credenza showed that. He dropped full length on the floor close enough to run his fingers along the narrow gap where the floorboards met the walls. He edged his way around the room, standing occasionally to shift furniture and his boxes before again sprawling full length on the floor.

He'd worked his way halfway around the room when he let out a shout of triumph. His fingers had closed over something round. His fingers flicked out his find onto the floorboards. A few inches away from his face lay a dark-brown button made from animal bone. He scrambled to his feet and sat on the bed. From the button's underside a few strands of cotton protruded, as if the button had been torn from its parent clothing.

Stafford considered the options. It was possible that the button had come from the coat of a passing traveller. A maid could have swept it into the gap between the boards several months ago. Yet the cotton strands indicated that it had been torn away, and not just dropped off and lost.

He stood up abruptly. The button was too big to come from women's clothing. More likely it came from a trail jacket or a topcoat of some sort. Where would he best get help to identify the garment from which it came? The general store was the obvious place. He pulled his lips back from his teeth. How would Josh Andrews react to him? Stafford caught sight of his own image in the mirror and shrugged. There was only one way to find out.

CHAPTER SIX

The next morning Stafford took his breakfast at the Chinaman's place a few minutes walk from the Majestic. From his table where he sat alone he could see through the open door men and women striding purposefully from store to store. He guessed that it was a trading day. How would the storekeepers react to the absence of the homesteaders' wagons? Stafford got up from his table and settled his bill with the celestial who bowed low in gratitude for the couple of extra coins Stafford added to the bill.

'You earned it, Mr Chang. You serve good chow.'

Stafford went out into the morning sunshine and crossed the street in the direction of the general store. The button he'd found in his room at the Majestic was in the pocket of his trail coat. He knew he'd have to pick his moment with Josh Andrews. Lucy's father, he'd heard, was a hot-tempered man who'd tried to attack Worley as Mackay was herding Tom into the jailhouse.

He put a finger to the brim of his hat as he passed Widow Brown on the boardwalk. 'Mrs Morgan is fine company,' the elderly woman told him. 'We've already had many delightful conversations.'

Stafford made the right noises before he moved on. He smiled to himself. Daisy Morgan had been taken through her story several times. He was confident she knew what to say in those 'delightful conversations'.

He reached the wide open door of the general store and peered inside. In front of a long broad counter a man in a dusty city suit was talking to a taller man behind the counter. Stafford recalled seeing the tall man at the entrance to the store. Josh Andrews. He overheard the customer settling his bill, and paused while the man picked up a box and turned towards the door. Stafford was conscious of the man eyeing him warily as they passed on the threshold. Inside, in front of high shelves, to Stafford's right, a young girl was filling boxes with iron nails.

Stafford approached the counter. 'Good day to you, Mr Andrews.'

Andrews glared at him for a second then turned to look towards the girl.

'Milly, you go out back 'til I call you,' he ordered.

'Yes, Mr Andrews,' she replied in a high voice. Her sharp black eyes never left Stafford as she crossed the store. Both men waited until the girl had gone behind the counter and stepped into the back room, closing the door behind her.

'My name is Stafford, Mr Andrews.'

Andrews glared across the counter. 'I know who you are. You're that damn fellow tryin' to save a blackguard's skin. I ain't talkin' with you an' I don' want you in my store.'

Stafford breathed in. This was going to be more difficult than he'd anticipated. 'I know it must be—'

'You know nothin'!' Andrews exploded.

He leaned so far across the broad counter that for a second Stafford thought the man was about to try and strike him. Instinctively, he stepped back out of Andrews' range, his muscles tensing.

'I told you once I don' want you here!' Andrews shouted. 'I got business to attend to!'

Andrews spun on his heel, showing only his back to Stafford, and went through the same door as the girl Milly, slamming the door behind him hard enough for it to shudder on its hinges.

Stafford swore under his breath. His

81

fingers tightened around the button in the pocket of his trail coat. Maybe if he tried another store he might get help. The Frenchman he'd noticed behind the counter of the dry goods store might help. He turned on his heel to quit the store and suddenly became aware of the small woman standing silently in the corner of the store. She must have entered quietly through the small door he'd not noticed before.

'Ma'am,' he said, acknowledging her. He headed for the door.

'Wait, Mr Stafford,' the woman called.

Stafford looked back. The woman was middle-aged, roughly the same age as Josh Andrews. The morning light caught the side of her face, and he could see that she'd once been pretty before the hard work of running the store had taken its toll.

'Mrs Andrews?' Stafford asked.

'Yes, Mr Stafford. I guess you're here about Lucy.'

'Yes, ma'am. But I don't aim to upset your husband.'

A faraway look came into her eyes, and for a moment she was silent.

'We loved Lucy dearly,' she said. 'Our boy was killed at Tupelo, an' it took a long time to get over the loss. Maybe we never have.

Lucy was all Mr Andrews had left. Aside from me, of course,' she added, almost as an afterthought.

'I can understand that, ma'am. I'm not here to cause trouble. I've been told Mr Worley was a good friend of your daughter.'

'He was. But Mr Andrews kept thinkin' about that Englishman a couple of years back. He sent Lucy presents. I made her throw them away.'

'Does the Englishman live hereabouts?'

Mrs Andrews shook her head. 'He moved on at the end of that summer. For Chicago, I heard.' She bit her lip. 'Lucy had a letter from Chicago only two weeks ago. I think the Englishman is coming back here. He's not a gentleman like your friend. Mr Andrews has his notions, but I'm sure Mr Worley was trying to keep Lucy calm and out of trouble.'

She lowered her eyes, her fingers picking nervously at the edge of her blue apron, forcing Stafford to step forward and strain his ears to catch her words.

'Poor Lucy was too forward from the day she put up her hair.' Mrs Andrews looked up at Stafford, grief etched across her face. 'If only she'd found a nice boy from here in Storm,' she said wistfully. 'But it was too late for that, an' now she's dead,' she said.

Stafford took the button from the pocket in his trail jacket, and held it towards her. 'Do you recognize this button, ma'am? It could be important.'

Mrs Andrews took the button from his hand, and looked at it carefully for a few moments.

'Yes,' she said finally. 'It's from a trail coat. Mr Andrews saw them in Cheyenne, and ordered a bundle. The coats were grey, I remember.'

Stafford looked around the store. 'Do you have any now?'

The woman shook her head. 'They were a good price, an' the timin' was right. They sold in a coupla weeks.'

'An' how many in the bundle sent from Cheyenne?'

'Fifty,' she replied.

Fifty! Stafford swore inwardly. Fifty men to chase down on what could well prove a waste of time. The search would take him weeks. Worley could be tried and hanged before he'd even found ten of the men who'd bought a coat. He took the button back.

'Thanks for your help, ma'am. I'm much obliged.'

'I hope you can help Mr Worley,' she said,

84

and turned away from him as the door behind the counter opened.

Stafford stepped out of the store onto the boardwalk. Had Andrews not reappeared he might have discovered the cause of the noisy quarrel between Lucy and Worley. He'd walk to the jailhouse and ask Tom, and make sure he got a straight answer.

He stepped out along the boardwalk, spurs jingling. He'd gone maybe twenty paces when he stopped, a wide smile across his face.

'Good day to you, Mrs Ross,' he said, grasping the brim of his hat for a moment. He glanced at the book in her hand. 'More reading for Tom?'

'Good day, Mr Stafford. Yes, I was going to deliver it after a small errand.'

'Then may we walk along together? I'm heading for the sheriff's office. We can see Tom together.'

Victoria Ross shook her head. 'Mr Mackay does not permit ladies to enter the jailhouse,' she said. Her lips tightened. 'We can vote in this territory, Mr Stafford, but we've still some way to go.'

Best not to answer that, Stafford decided. Instead, he held out his hand. 'Then allow me to deliver the book for you,' he said.

'Yes, that's kind.' She handed the book to Stafford who glanced down at the title but made no comment.

'Shall we see you later today, Mr Stafford?' Seeing Stafford's puzzled frown, she explained. 'Storm Creek was established twenty years ago today. The townsfolk gather and remember the early pioneers. There's music, steers are roasted, and a bonfire is lit.'

Stafford remembered the huge pile of wood and stuff at the end of Main Street when he'd been waiting for Bagley's buckboard. 'I'm not sure I'm fit company for a party, Mrs Ross.'

Victoria Ross inclined her chin an inch.

'Neither am I, Mr Stafford. But Amy Brand is a good friend of mine. If you wish to meet Elias Brand this is your opportunity. I'll be at the schoolhouse at four. Maybe you'd be kind enough to escort me.'

Her face had turned pink as she uttered her last request, but she held her head high, continuing to look directly at Stafford. Determination showed in the set of her lips. 'We both know Tom Worley might hang, Mr Stafford. If he's to be freed there's no time for false modesty.'

Stafford pushed the book through the bars.

'The latest from Mr Dickens,' he said. 'Mrs Ross must have money.'

'She has,' Worley said. 'An' she spends it for the good of Storm Creek. I'm told that nine years ago she built the schoolhouse with her own money. She had Mr Mackay chase the children to her classroom and the town has never looked back.'

Stafford sat on the chair he'd fetched from the end of the passageway, and examined Worley's face. The strain was becoming more evident each day, Stafford realized. He could see it in his friend's eyes.

'You ever own a grey trail coat, Tom?' Stafford asked.

Worley shook his head. 'Haven't worn a trail coat in ten years.' He managed a weak smile. 'Not the right clothes for a respectable lawyer.'

Stafford ignored his puzzled look. 'OK, so what was the big quarrel with Lucy Andrews about?'

Worley hesitated for a moment then shook his head. 'Aw, hell! The poor girl's dead now, so what does it matter?'

Stafford remained silent, waiting.

'Lucy was taking laudanum,' Worley said. 'I was trying to stop her.'

Stafford frowned. 'Was she sick?'

Worley shook his head. 'No. She'd become addicted.'

'Where was she gettin' the opium?'

'I don't know. I tried to make her tell me, but she wouldn't. Doc Mayerling told me it wasn't him. I'd planned to find out but–' He broke off, and shrugged. 'I finished up here.'

Stafford changed the subject. 'You heard of an Englishman hereabouts. Friend of Lucy's?'

Worley shook his head. 'Coupla home-steaders were from England, I think. But they were good family men and moved on some months back.'

Stafford got to his feet. 'Looks as if I'm gonna meet Elias Brand today,' he said. 'You wanna say anythin' 'bout that?'

Worley thought for a moment. 'He's not a well man but in some ways he's as sharp as a cavalry sword. In other ways he's living in the past. He can't face the fact that times are changing, and the big ranchers have to live with the homesteaders arriving.' Worley's mouth twisted. 'But he's hired some real bad no-goods, Luke. Feller by the name of Hard-man who runs 'em is the one to watch.'

Stafford paused. Hardman? He knew the name. Then he dismissed the notion. There must be a thousand Hardmans in the territory. 'Enjoy the book, Tom,' he said. 'Take your mind off things.'

Stafford pushed open the door to the school-room. Back at the Majestic he'd opened one of his boxes to dig out fresh clothes. Fifty cents had a maid running to his room with damp cloths and a sizzling hot iron. He hoped Victoria Ross would approve. Then he grinned. He hadn't sought a woman's approval since the day his mother died.

Victoria Ross was at her table examining a slate. Her dog, Ruff, got up from the floor where he'd been lying beside her and walked towards Stafford. He put out a hand to touch the dog's head. The animal looked up at him, his tongue lolling, before appearing to lose any further interest and making its way back to the desk.

Victoria Ross turned the timepiece held to her coat by a gold pin and glanced down. 'Forgive me, Mr Stafford. I'm late.' She held up the slate. 'Come and see this. You might find it interesting.'

Stafford crossed the schoolroom to look at the slate. He frowned. Chalk marks showed some sort of writing. 'What in tarnation is that?'

'Mirror writing,' Victoria Ross said. 'One

of my girls writes normally with her right hand, and does this with her left. Doctor Mayerling is most interested in her mind.' She held the slate closer to Stafford. 'You can see the writing's back to front.'

Stafford was silent for a few seconds staring at the slate. 'Back to front,' he said slowly. 'Mebbe that's the answer.'

Victoria Ross raised quizzical eyebrows. 'Excuse me?'

Stafford stepped back from her, turning his hat in his hands. 'Mebbe I'm the one who's been thinkin' back to front. I've been assumin', same as Tom Worley, that the killin' o' Lucy Andrews was set up to get Tom out o' the way. I've had the notion before, an' I'm beginnin' to reckon there's somethin' to it. Suppose that Lucy was the real target an' the killer was just usin' the quarrel she had with Tom as a cover?'

'But why would anyone want to kill a young girl like Lucy? And in such a violent way?'

Stafford looked thoughtful. Finally, he shook his head.

'Can't think o' anythin' at all, ma'am,' he said. He held out his arm. 'Mebbe I'll think o' somethin' after I've met Elisha Brand.'

Stafford guessed that preparations for the town's party were underway as soon as he stepped out from the schoolhouse with Mrs Ross on his arm. A buzz of excited voices sounded from the direction of Main Street. There were the sounds of hammers being swung against metal and the rasp of wood being sawn. As the couple neared the end of the street Stafford saw the carcasses of several steers being offloaded from a wagon.

'Mr Brand always provides the supper,' Victoria Ross said. 'He'll be here already to watch over arrangements.'

They reached the open space beyond the boardwalk and the bathhouse where the bonfire was to be lit and the steers roasted. A few yards from the stacked timber a group of people stood talking. Victoria Ross steered Stafford in their direction. As they neared the group a young woman turned in their direction. Her blue silk dress was obviously expensive, as was the light shawl around her shoulders meant to ward off the cool air of the early evening. Blonde ringlets bounced on her pale forehead as she stepped towards them.

'Victoria! I'm so pleased you came. I've much to tell you.' She turned to Stafford. 'Mr Stafford, I guess.'

91

He gave a small bow, at the same time taking off his Stetson. 'An' I guess you must be Miss Amy Brand.'

As Amy Brand smiled her acknowledgement Stafford became aware that the older man of the group had turned to stare hard at him. Black eyes, as hard as coal, examined him from head to foot. Elisha Brand, owner of the Double B, Stafford guessed.

The rancher was dressed in the style of a cowboy about to work cattle out on the range. But instead of a cowboy's rough working clothes he wore soft woollen pants tucked into gleaming leather boots, cavalry fashion. His coat, styled like a trail coat, was made of soft leather, and on his head he wore a cream-coloured Stetson. He spoke loudly, his tone aggressive, across the several yards that separated the two men.

'So you're the Stafford who's a friend of that blackguard Worley.'

Stafford didn't reply immediately, returning Brand's stare. 'Yes. I'm a friend of Tom Worley,' he said finally. No sense in getting into a fight before he'd even had the chance to size up Brand. He touched Victoria Ross lightly on the arm. 'Why don't you hear what Miss Amy has to say to you?'

'Yes, do come and talk, Victoria,' Amy

Brand said. She put a hand on Brand's arm. 'Please, Father. Remember what I asked.'

She didn't wait for Brand's answer. Instead, taking the older woman's arm she led her away. Brand waited until the women were out of earshot before moving closer to Stafford. The three men who'd been in the group when Stafford and Victoria Ross arrived, drifted away.

'An' you're aimin' to get Worley out of jail, if I've heard aright.'

'Yeah, that's about it,' Stafford said.

Brand's mouth set, his eyes hard. 'You're in Storm Creek now, Stafford. A man kills a gal and he ends up on a rope.'

Stafford nodded. 'We do the same for horse-thieves back where I come from.'

Brand's face turned scarlet. 'You talkin' 'bout that fool son o' mine? That boy ain't got the brains of a jack-rabbit. If Jamie had lived things would be different! God help the Double B when I've gone!' He thrust his face towards Stafford. 'You listen hard! You're in cattle country now, an' don't you forget it. I hear you linin' up with those homesteaders an' I'll bury you. Goddamn nesters who gut the range with their ploughs. The Double B needs all the grass it can get, an' I aim to take it back!'

'You're fightin' time, Brand. The home-steaders have legal rights. In a year or two there'll be a lot more law than Mackay 'round these parts.'

Stafford, his gaze unflinchingly on Brand, was nevertheless aware that their confront-ation was beginning to attract the attention of bystanders. Brand seemed oblivious of the stares, or didn't care.

'We got all the law we need!' Brand's voice had risen to a shout. 'We got an honest sheriff who knows a killer when he sees one.' Spittle flew from the man's mouth. 'You ain't back in Boston. In Storm we got no need for a fancy police agent or whatever you call yourself.'

Brand's final words caught Stafford un-awares, but before he could reply someone spoke behind him.

'Yeah, what do you call yourself nowadays, Luke?'

Stafford turned on his heel. Immediately, Brand's mention of Boston became clearer. A tall, heavily built man stood with his hands loosely at his sides. Stafford glanced at the man's left hip, but Hardman was unarmed as would be all the men at the gathering.

'Howdy, Jack,' Stafford said. 'It's been some time.' He moved his head in Brand's

94

direction. 'I guess you changed your line o' business.'

Hardman shrugged. 'Feller's gotta make a dollar.' He looked past Stafford to the rancher. 'Mr Brand, how 'bout me an' Stafford here goin' for a beer. Mebbe I can talk some sense into him.'

Brand nodded. 'Remember what I said, Stafford,' he said abruptly. 'I don't warn a man more than once. Worley found that out the hard way.'

He turned his back and walked away in the direction of his daughter and Victoria Ross.

'C'mon, Luke,' Hardman said. 'The ladies'll wait.'

Hardman walked across to a trestle table where George, the saloon keeper, was setting up his stall. George, Stafford saw, seemed only too keen to pass over a couple of beers without payment.

'There's a quiet spot,' Hardman said, and led the way beyond the pile of timber around which some of the townsfolk were setting faggots ready to start the fire. Out of earshot of any of the townsfolk the two men sipped at their beers for a few moments.

'OK, Jack, I'm listenin',' Stafford said finally.

'We were a good team once, you an' me,' Hardman said. 'Sure, we had our differences, but what happened between us is dead an' gone. We can be a team agin, Luke. But this time we ain't gonna be workin' for wages. We can make money.' His eyes gleamed. 'Lots of it, Luke! It's there for the takin'!'

Stafford drank more of his beer. 'Where's it comin' from?'

'The Double B! Brand's a sick man. He's been failin' since his other boy Jamie, got hisself killed. That brat, Frank, ain't up to it!' His hand clutched at Stafford's arm. 'Work with me, Luke. I got men with me. The cowboys ain't gonna be trouble. The ranch could be ourn for the takin'.' Hardman nodded in the direction of Amy Brand. 'She's lookin' for a husband, Luke. I know she ain't taken a fancy to me an' I tried hard enough. You're a fine-lookin' feller. You can get to courtin' her.'

Hardman's eyes, a metallic blue, were bright with desperate hope. He was a man, Stafford realized, not getting any younger who thought he saw one last chance of making it big. Stafford looked back steadily over the rim of his beer mug. Mentally, he replayed what Hardman had said. Five years

96

had passed since they'd worked together, the two of them, alongside Amos Jackson. When Jackson was killed and the team split up, he'd had his doubts. At the time he wasn't sure that expressing those doubts to the distinguished man who employed them was the right move to make. But now he was sure. Hardman was still the same low-down son of a bitch he always was. Even while taking Brand's money for doing his dirty work he was plotting against him.

'An' what about the homesteaders?' Stafford said.

Hardman shrugged. 'The few that's left ain't gonna be a problem. Sure, I heard they'd done some soldierin', but they ain't organized. I'm aimin' to clear 'em out afore summer's finished.'

Stafford drained the last of his beer, his eyes hard. 'Then you've got a problem, Jack. I ain't in town only to get Tom Worley out o' jail: I'm linin' up with the homesteaders, an' all.' He shoved the empty beer mug into Hardman's hand. 'You're on the opposite side to me, Jack. Make sure it don't get you killed.'

CHAPTER SEVEN

Two days had passed since Stafford's meeting with Elisha Brand and his clash with Jack Hardman. For the last forty-eight hours he'd been holed up with a dozen of the homesteaders in the main cabin of Theo Morgan and his family

The ex-soldiers hadn't forgotten how to be patient while waiting for action. Before sunup they'd roused themselves and washed at the well in the starry darkness before listening to what Stafford had to say. He'd made sure they all had coffee before he'd begun to tell them what he'd been turning over in his mind during the night.

'We give it one more day,' he'd told them. 'Brand would have gotten word by now to have him thinkin' this place is empty for a few days. If he's a mind to send his no-goods he'll not wait much longer.'

'It's worth waitin' for, Cap'n,' had said the man who'd already donned his blue woollen hat for the day. His name, Stafford had learned, was Miller. There had been noises of support from the others for Miller's remarks, and Stafford and Bagley had exchanged satisfied glances.

Now, Stafford stood at the window looking north, deliberating in his mind if the trap he'd set would be sprung before the men ran out of patience and decided they had to return to work their own homesteads.

He glanced over his shoulder. Some of the men were playing cards, one was carving animal bone, a couple were reading mail-order catalogues of farming equipment. How long would they continue to be settled?

His head swung around sharply as the noise of a galloping horse reached his ears. The men must've heard it, too, as cards, carvings, books and catalogues were thrown down. Men reached for long guns and sidearms.

The galloping horse bore down on the cabin. 'It's Jenkins,' shouted Bagley 'He musta seen somethin'!'

Stafford strode to the door and threw it open. He saw Jenkins heave back on his mount's reins, bringing the big roan to a sudden halt a few feet from where Stafford stood.

'Bunch o' riders comin' this way, Cap'n,' Jenkins said, his breathing heavy. 'Reckon they're what we're waitin' for.'

'How many?' Stafford rapped out.

'Six, mebbe seven.'

'Get your mount in the barn with the rest o' the horses,' Stafford ordered. He spun on his heel to address the men, gathered in a group behind him. 'You know your positions. Get to 'em!'

The men moved quickly around the cabin, a pair to each opening in the timber walls. They half-closed the heavy shutters, allowing space to aim their long guns while protecting themselves if they were fired upon. One man stood at the centre of the room. In front of him were extra long guns and boxes of ammunition to be supplied to any marksman who called for a loaded weapon. One man stood ready to climb a ladder should any attacker attempt to set fire to the timbers of the roof.

Stafford waited until Jenkins had settled his horse and run back from the barn. With Jenkins safely inside the cabin he slammed the door shut and barred it with a length of stout timber. He moved quickly to stand alongside Bagley. Through the barely open shutter he saw the group of riders appear on the high ground to the north. The riders halted, and Stafford guessed they were looking for signs of life around the homestead. They were too far away to identify but he was willing to wager Jenkins was right. They were Hardman's gunslingers carrying out Brand's orders. As he watched, a solitary rider crested the hills some distance to the right of the group. Stafford frowned. What was going on here?

'Spyglass, Sergeant!' Immediately, Stafford swung around to Bagley.

'Joe, I–'

Bagley cut him off, amused. 'Like old times, Cap'n!' Then his face set, and he thrust the brass telescope into Stafford's outstretched hand.

'Spyglass, Cap'n!'

Stafford raised the telescope to his eye. Two twists of the barrel and he brought the lone figure into focus. For a moment he was puzzled by the appearance of the rider, shadowed eyes in a long white face. He had a mental flash of one of the men who'd attacked him in Worley's office. Then Stafford realized the man's face was covered with some sort of cloth. As he watched, the man's mount turned until the animal was side on to Stafford. He moved the spyglass a fraction. The rider was wearing his sidearm on the left hip. Hardman, Stafford was sure.

'Hardman's just givin' the orders. I reckon

101

he ain't gonna take part.' He looked over his shoulder at the men around the room. 'Remember, I ain't aimin' for a bloodbath here. We're just gonna teach 'em a lesson.'

'Here they come, Cap'n!' Bagley shouted. He jumped forward and pulled the shutter half-closed, bringing up his Winchester to aim at the oncoming riders.

'Hold your fire until I give the order.'

Stafford kept his eyes on the line of riders strung out across the open ground. They'd reached maybe a quarter of a mile from the cabin. With his naked eye he could just make out that all the riders had their faces covered in the same way as Hardman's.

'Now wouldn't that be somethin',' he said softly to himself.

He raised the spyglass, swinging it to and fro along the line, his fingers twisting the barrel to keep the oncoming riders in focus. He stopped suddenly, and let out a short bark of triumph. He'd guessed right.

Almost at the same time a single rider broke away from the line. Stafford saw him slow his mount, his head down, leaning to the side of his horse away from Stafford.

'He's gonna fire us, Cap'n!' Jenkins yelled, as the rider turned his horse's head. In his hand he now held up a burning brand.

Stafford saw him dig his heels into his mount, and the animal sped forward.

'He's aimin' for my barn.' Morgan shouted.

Stafford swore. Whatever he'd hoped for, he wasn't about to risk Morgan's barn and the men's horses. 'Corporal Jenkins.'

'Cap'n.'

'Stop him.'

'Cap'n!' Jenkins acknowledged the order.

There came the rough rasp of a Winchester being readied. Stafford watched as the rider reached a spot fifty yards from the barn. There was the crack of a long gun, the sound bouncing around the walls of the cabin. Almost simultaneously the rider was hurled from his saddle, the burning brand spinning from his grasp to fall harmlessly to the ground among the damp bunch and buffalo grass. Grey smoke mixed with yellow flames.

The line of riders, a couple of hundred yards behind the dead man, reined in their mounts and halted. A few seconds later in response to a waved hand from the rider of a big roan they drew their long guns from their rifle scabbards. They kicked their horses forward, the animals breaking into a gallop as the masked men rode down on their cabin.

'Fire over their heads when ready!' Bagley

ordered, following the plan he and Stafford had agreed upon. Instantly, there was a volley of shots from a dozen long guns. The line of galloping horses broke, and their riders swerved away in half-a-dozen directions.

'Guess they thought there was only one man here,' one of the men shouted. Laughter broke out as the men hooted and whistled.

'Silence!' Bagley roared. 'It ain't over yet.'

'Corporal Jenkins! Shoot the roan,' Stafford ordered. 'I want the man alive.'

'Cap'n!'

For maybe twenty yards the roan was shielded from view behind another horse. Then the two riders divided and the roan was clearly visible, moving away fast. Still Jenkins didn't fire. Stafford swore under his breath. As he did so, Jenkins's Winchester fired once, ratcheted and fired again. As the shots rang out the roan lost control of its legs and staggered like a saloon drunk before plunging to the ground. The rider was hurled clear of the dying horse and sent rolling across the ground until he came to stop and lay still.

'They come back for him, we stop 'em,' Stafford ordered.

But the riders never looked back, spurring on their mounts to ride north, racing towards the high ground where they'd first appeared. Stafford watched them for several minutes. Then, satisfied, he strode to the door, and threw the bar aside.

'Gimme a hand, Joe.'

Keeping wary eyes on the disappearing riders, the two men crossed the ground to halt beside the fallen rider.

'He's alive, Cap'n. What we gonna do with him?' Bagley asked, looking down at the man. As he spoke the fallen man began to stir.

Stafford bent to tear away the mask that covered the man's face. He saw now that it was a simple flour bag, holes cut in the material for the eyes and the mouth.

The man looked up at Stafford, fear showing in his eyes. Stafford's mouth twitched.

'Howdy, Frank,' he said. 'You're goin' to jail, an' this time you're stayin' there.'

Mackay's eyes bulged with shock. 'Say that agin, Stafford!'

Stafford stepped a further couple of paces into the sheriff's office, spreading both hands on Mackay's desk, and leaning forward. 'I'm tellin' you again, Sheriff. I got one dead no-good, and Frank Brand in a wagon outside. You wanna take a look?'

He stepped back as Mackay jumped to his

feet, and crossed his office to peer through the window. Over Mackay's shoulder, Stafford saw Joe Bagley holding the reins of his big grey, raise his hand to acknowledge the sheriff.

'What the hell you been up to, Stafford?'

Stafford took a chair as Mackay regained his seat behind his desk. In a few rapid words he described the events of the morning. When he'd finished Mackay swore loudly.

'The homesteads are outside my jurisdiction! I tol' you that the other day.'

Stafford pulled the map he'd been given by Worley from an inside pocket of his trail coat. He opened it and placed it on the desk in front of Mackay. With a finger he pointed out Morgan's homestead. Between two lines showing the corner of the homestead an area was shaded with black ink.

'You wanna measure that, Mr Mackay? Corner of Morgan's place is in your territory.'

Mackay ignored the map, his face set, staring directly at Stafford.

'Your story don' stand up,' he said. 'Six or seven riders, all masked. Yet you pick out Frank Brand. How come that happen?'

Stafford waited a few seconds before replying. Mackay, he decided, was not only honest he was smart. 'His fancy boots,' he said. 'He was wearin' 'em that day I brought him in.'

Mackay didn't reply directly. Instead, he looked down at the map.

'I'll take your word about Morgan's place. But let's get something clear between us: I ain't stickin' Frank Brand in jail. I've kept the peace in this town for a long time. Time was, we had men in this town who rustled Double B cattle for a grub stake. I got rid of 'em. This town has prospered 'cos I've kept Elisha Brand friendly. An' puttin' his only son in jail ain't gonna help one goddamned bit.'

Stafford looked over his shoulder towards the stove. 'You mind if I get some coffee?'

Mackay frowned as if thrown off balance by Stafford's polite request.

'Help yourself,' he said.

'You want one?'

Mackay's puzzled frown deepened. 'Yeah, sure. Always ready for coffee.'

The two men remained silent while Stafford poured coffee and carried the tin mugs to place them on Mackay's desk. Stafford sat down, and fishing below the open neck of his woollen shirt he took out a small linen bag of Bull Durham. With papers from the top pocket of his vest he deftly rolled a couple of smokes. He handed one to Mackay, and lit them both with a match. The sheriff took the smoke, his wary eyes showing he knew that this hadn't suddenly turned into social call.

Finally, Stafford spoke. 'You know of a feller the name o' Lew Walker?'

Mackay nodded. 'Sure, top lawman in Cheyenne.'

'Supposin' I rode to Cheyenne an' tol' him you'd admitted that the raid on Morgan's homestead was within your jurisdiction but you'd refused to do anythin' about it?'

Mackay took a draw of his smoke, thinking. Then he chuckled.

'Walker's a top man. You ain't gonna get near him. An' even if you did, you think he's gonna take the word of a stranger agin me? I tol' you once, Stafford. I been 'round Storm for nigh on ten years; Walker knows my name.'

'You know anythin' about Walker?'

Mackay shrugged. 'Not a lot, I guess. I know he was a top Pinkerton agent.'

A slow smile began to spread across Stafford's face. Mackay was a quick thinker, Stafford had to give him his due, as he watched the confident look in Mackay's face drain away to be replaced with red-faced anger as the truth dawned on him.

'Fer Chris'sakes, Stafford!' Mackay

exploded. 'You come into my town you shoulda made yourself known. What the hell do the Pinkertons want in Storm Creek?'

Stafford waved a hand in the air. 'Relax, Mr Mackay. This ain't a Pinkerton job. I came here to visit Tom Worley that's all.' He leaned forward in his chair. 'Sheriff, I ain't got no argument with you. You're doin' your job as you see it. But what I said still goes. The Brands are tied in with the killin' o' Lucy Andrews in some way. Frank Brand's broken the law. You ain't crossin' any lines by puttin' him in jail, an' it's gonna stir up what's goin' on 'round here.'

Mackay pulled his lips back from his teeth. The expression on his face showed clearly that he was torn between his instinct to keep the town quiet and on the side of Elisha Brand. Yet at the same time he was being forced to recognize that Stafford had the law on his side. A law he, Mackay had sworn to uphold. With a grunt of exasperation Mackay stood up and reached for the bunch of keys that hung from a hook on the wall.

'I ain't lookin' forward to the next few days,' he said. 'I hope I get to live through 'em.'

Stafford took the steps from Main Street up

to Galton's store two at a time. Events were moving in his direction. He could feel it just as he had many times before. Sure, he hadn't yet discovered who had killed Lucy Andrews but the Double B and Storm Creek were being shaken around like the coloured pieces of paper in the kaleidoscope he'd seen once at a carnival down in Texas. When people and events were shaken around enough, then truth came out.

He pushed open the door of Galton's store. Galton wasn't at his desk but the door at the rear of the room was ajar.

'Harry! You here?' Stafford called.

Galton appeared through the open door, wiping his hands on a rag. Stafford guessed he must have been working in the back room seeing that he wore a stained blue apron over his city trousers and silk vest. Galton turned around and tossed the rag into the back room out of sight.

'Good day, Luke. You here for the pictures?'

'They ready?'

Galton nodded. 'Yeah, I think they're what you want.'

He walked to a large cabinet and opened the top drawer. Glancing down at his hands first to check they were clean Galton pulled out three photographs. He carried them across to his desk, used one hand to push away an accounts book, and laid the photographs alongside each other.

'C'mon an' take a look,' Galton said.

Stafford joined him at the desk and bent to examine Galton's work. All the photographs showed the body of Lucy Andrews from the curve of her shoulders to the top of her head. At centre in each photograph the lines of the knife cut across her throat were clearly shown.

'This is what I wanted, Harry. You've sure earned your money,' he said.

'I gotta tell you I was lucky,' Galton said. 'Took a lot o' foolin' around. Smallwood almost swooned.' He hesitated for a second. 'You gonna tell me what you're aimin' to do with these? Folks see these, an' I ain't gonna be too popular in town.'

'Nobody's gonna see 'em, Harry.'

'So why'd you want 'em?'

'I don't know, Harry, an' that's the truth.' Stafford smiled grimly. 'Coupla years back a doctor from Edinburgh, Scotland, came to Boston. Name o' Joseph Bell, I recall. Told us we had to collect every fact about a crime, even if it don't seem to mean much at the time. That's what I'm doin' now.'

Galton's grin looked a little forced. 'I sure hope I'm on the side of righteousness.'

Stafford laughed out loud. 'I ain't sure I can claim that, Harry!' His expression became serious. 'But I aim to get Tom Worley out of that jail.' His mouth twitched. 'Anyways, I guess I ain't the only one that's mebbe hidin' somethin' with that stuff o' yourn I saw in the saloon.'

Galton opened his mouth to reply when the door was flung open.

Victoria Ross stood at the threshold. Without haste, Galton picked up the photographs from the desk, and slid them back into the cabinet drawer out of sight.

'Luke, I've found something!' Victoria Ross's breath was short, and her face flushed with excitement.

'Tell me,' he said. He saw her eyes shift to Galton. 'Harry's with us,' he said.

With both men listening intently she described what she'd found, only pausing when first Stafford and then Galton asked her questions. When she'd finished talking Stafford stepped forward to look over her shoulder up at the sky

'Too late, now,' he said. 'We'll ride out in the morning. Meet me at the livery an hour after sun-up.'

CHAPTER EIGHT

The high wide doors were already open when Stafford got to the livery half an hour after sun-up. As he stepped into the barn the familiar tang of horseflesh, straw, and oats came to his nostrils. He moved down the centre of the barn. Horses shifted as he reached level with their stalls, their hoofs rustling straw. A couple of the animals snorted loudly as though impatient to be out for the day.

'Mr Fellowes! You up an' about?' Stafford called out.

A tall, gaunt man clad in blue denim emerged from one of the stalls over to Stafford's right. In his hand he held a two-pronged fork, wisps of straw hanging from the tines.

'Sure am, Mr Stafford,' Fellowes called. 'Got that fine hoss o' yourn saddled up just as you paid me for.'

Stafford thrust his hand into his pocket as Fellowes drew closer. 'Coupla whiskeys extra, you saddle up Mrs Ross's horse.' He handed a coin to Fellowes.

The liveryman cackled with pleasure, showing teeth stained brown from chewing tobacco. He held out his hand and took the coin.

'That's mighty kinda you. I'll take them whiskeys.' He pointed over Stafford's shoulder. 'But the lady's hoss is all saddled up.'

Stafford turned to look in the direction Fellowes was pointing. In a stall on the other side of the barn he saw a big chestnut mare with a blazed face. Stafford frowned as he saw the chestnut's rig.

'Mrs Ross ride 'cross the horse?'

Fellowes let out another cackle of laughter. 'Sure she does! Shocked all the ladies of the town she first came here.' His face split into a brown, toothy grin. 'Afore that Englishwoman sent her fancy clothes Mrs Ross had to mount in here an' ride out. Other fellers in here with their hosses an' she had to walk outa town afore she could climb on Lizzie. That's her chestnut,' Fellowes added, his expression showing that in his view only a fine lady would call a chestnut mare by the name of Lizzie.

Stafford nodded in apparent agreement, keeping a straight face. Victoria Ross was quite a woman, he decided. A thought came to him which had been on the edge of his mind for several days. Why hadn't she remarried? He'd always been told that ladies were in short supply out here in the West. Plenty of other women, of course, the saloons were full of them.

When men were sending back East for brides by mail order, it was puzzling that an attractive lady like Mrs Ross could have remained a widow for long. Something else occurred to him: was Victoria Ross the wife-to-be of Tom Worley? His friend's words came back to him. 'She has no husband'. Had Tom, the lawyer, been playing with words, ducking the question?

'Luke! So deep in thought for early in the morning!'

Stafford spun on his heel. A smiling Victoria Ross stood a few paces from him. In her hand she was carrying a short riding crop with a beaten silver head. Below her tight woollen jacket she was wearing a calf-length skirt over silk pleated trousers which fell in frills over black shiny boots.

Stafford thought she was the most handsome woman he'd ever seen and was almost tempted to tell her so. Maybe, he thought, wryly, it must have been showing in his face, as delicate spots of pink appeared on her high cheekbones.

'I've seen that handsome riding dress before,' he said, hastily, to cover his confusion. 'Down in Truckee, Colorado.'

Her eyes sparkled with pleasure. 'On a fine Englishwoman, Miss Isobel Bird!'

'Hey, that's right.' Stafford laughed at the memory. 'Some of us down there got roped in for a wild-cattle roundup. Miss Bird made sure she was part of it an' rode like a demon. Tol' some of the men they wouldn't last a day in the hunting field back in England.'

'She visited here last year and shocked the town riding like a man. That made two of us. When she went back to England she sent me these clothes.' Victoria Ross made a mock flourish with her riding crop. '"The American Lady's Mountain Dress" she said it was called.'

'It looks fine, Victoria,' Stafford said.

If she even raised an eyebrow at the use of her forename, he decided, he'd apologize for being over-familiar. But she said nothing and continued to smile, looking directly into his eyes.

'We'll have to get goin',' he said. 'Lizzie's ready to go.'

He turned and walked over to where his palomino was nuzzling at a haynet. He opened the half-door and moved alongside the horse to unhook the reins from the horn. He turned the horse and led the animal out of the stall and down the length of the barn, pausing halfway to wait for Victoria Ross and her mare.

Outside the light was brighter as the sun began to make its mark on the town. Sitting on the ground looking eagerly in their direction was the dog he'd first seen in the schoolhouse. He turned to Victoria, as he was now thinking of her, to see her emerge from the barn leading Lizzie.

'Ruff comin' with us?'

'Of course,' she said. 'Without Ruff I'd have ridden straight past.'

Stafford shrugged inwardly. Some of the men he'd ridden with over the years might have had something to say if they'd seen him riding along with a sheepman's dog. He grinned at nothing in particular. What the hell! There was a serious aim to their ride, but right now he knew he wouldn't be anywhere else. He turned to mount his palomino as Victoria walked her mare towards the mounting stone. He turned in his saddle unintentionally catching a glimpse of a long silk-clad leg before Victoria adjusted her skirt.

'How long you reckon this'll take?' Stafford asked.

'Maybe two hours, a little less,' she said.

He nodded, and turned the head of his palomino. 'Let's take a look at this cabin you've found.'

They rode alongside each other for about half an hour at a gentle trot, not saying much, both enjoying the clear morning air of the early Wyoming summer. Ruff ran back and forward, attending to interesting scents as he kept a wary eye on the rear hoofs of the two horses. After a while Stafford could control his curiosity no longer.

'You mind my askin' what brought you to Storm Creek,' he asked.

She turned her head to look at him, not answering immediately, but she appeared then to make a decision as she gave a brief nod.

'Because I have money and city manners people in Storm think I'm a fine lady.' She smiled. 'I'm not. I was governess to the six children of a wealthy banker back East.' Her smile faded. 'That's the fate, Luke, of educated young girls from families without money. And the life of a governess is not always a happy one. Part of the family, yes, but also a servant and often reminded of that status.'

She was silent while the two horses covered a hundred yards or so. Just as Stafford was about to say something, she spoke.

'The children's mother died,' she continued. 'Mr Ross was almost broken with grief and worry about the future of his children.' She paused, and looked away towards the horizon ahead. 'He asked me to marry him, and although I was very young I accepted. He died five years later.' She pressed her lips together. 'I soon discovered that polite society had only accepted me because of him. His sister took the children and I decided to come out West and start again. I've been here almost ten years, and I intend to stay.'

Stafford had almost to bite his tongue to prevent him asking further questions but while his brain was racing to think of something appropriate to say he was saved by Victoria's smile and the shadows clearing from her eyes as she looked across at him.

'That's my story, Luke! What's yours?'

'Nothin' much to tell,' he said. 'Army in the War then I went to work for Pinkerton's. Pay's good, an' in a coupla years I can hand in my badge and go work in a dry goods store or somethin'.'

The clear air was disturbed by Victoria's peals of laughter. 'You in a dry goods store, Luke!' She attempted a gruff voice, not very successfully. 'An' how many bolts of cotton is it today, Mrs Brown.'

Stafford grinned. 'OK. Maybe not in a dry goods store.'

Victoria became serious. 'Was that brute Hardman a Pinkerton man?'

Stafford nodded. 'I worked with him for a while, afore Pinkerton broke up our team.'

'Why was that?'

Stafford had been watching the trail ahead, looking for the large stand of cotton-woods that Victoria had described the previous evening. He turned his head to look at her.

'There were three of us. The other was a really good man, Amos Jackson. We were all different men, mebbe that's what made us a good team. Amos was devout; he saw his job trackin' down no-goods as the job he did to help good people.' His mouth set. 'Hard-man ain't like that. We were in this town in Kansas, and had to question a really good family whose son had taken the owlhoot trail with three others.'

Stafford blew out air. 'The family had a

young gal, real pretty. She thought we were all like the men she'd read about in books. Brave gunfighters, heroes on white horses, you know the sorta thing.' His eyes became flinty. 'Hardman took advantage of her, and Amos was wild with anger, threatening to report him to the office in Chicago.'

'What happened?' Victoria asked soberly.

'We tracked the no-goods to a cabin twenty miles from the town. There was a gunfight and Amos died. I could never prove what I suspected, but I sure wasn't goin' to work with Hardman any more.' He looked forward along the trail suddenly. 'Is that the stand of cottonwoods?'

'That's the one,' she said.

They both dug their heels into the side of their mounts, urging the horses forward. Behind them, Ruff looked up suddenly from nosing the grass and broke into a run after them. Ten minutes later, following Victoria's directions from the previous evening Stafford reined in his palomino at a gap in the outer ring of cottonwoods.

'This is where Ruff disappeared yesterday,' Victoria explained. 'I waited but when he didn't return I went into the trees to find him. We can take the horses a little of the way, but then we'll have to make our way on foot. From there the cabin is only about a hundred yards.'

Stafford looked around, sizing up the situation. 'So if anyone's in the cabin now, we should see their mount first.' He looked around again, judging the ground. 'There could be another gap that leads to the cabin.'

She shook her head. 'When I really thought Ruff was lost I rode all around the trees. This is the only way in.'

Stafford looked again at the gap between the trees. 'An' I reckon you could pass here every day an' not know about the cabin.'

Ducking his head to avoid the low branches he led the way into the dark shadowy spaces between the trees, Victoria close behind him, the dog weaving his way through the closely packed trees. After fifty yards, when the morning sun was blotted out by the thick branches above, Stafford was forced to dismount so he could heave back a thick, low-lying branch that barred their only way forward.

'I was on foot from here,' Victoria explained.

They made maybe another hundred yards before Stafford held up his hand. The trunks of the cottonwoods, some close to each other, some dead and fallen to the spongy ground made further progress on horseback impossible. They both dismounted.

'There could be somebody in the cabin,' Stafford said.

'I'm goin' ahead. You gonna be OK here?'

'I always have this when I'm out riding.'

Victoria reached beneath her skirt. Again, Stafford caught a tantalizing glimpse of a silk-clad leg. But that was not what caused his surprise.

'What in tarnation you got there?'

He gazed at the small multi-barrelled sidearm she held firmly before her.

'Five .22 shots. All at once if needs be.' She glanced down. 'It's called a Ladies Companion.'

Stafford nodded. He'd heard of such a gun but he'd never seen one before. 'You ever fired it?'

'I've killed rats and I practise every week.'

Stafford grinned. Some schoolmarm! 'OK. You hear any shootin' you skedaddle outa here. I'll be fine,' he added, seeing her expression change. 'The cabin's probably empty. You come up when I call you.' He glanced down at the dog seated beside his mistress. 'An' keep Ruff quiet.'

She nodded. 'I understand.'

He turned, and began to move carefully

between the trees, his Colt held loosely by his side. After fifty yards the trees began to thin, some on the ground having been felled to make a rough track. Twenty-five yards further along the track the outline of a cabin appeared between the trees. He half crouched, moving quickly from one cottonwood to another. Ten more yards and he reached the inner ring of trees surrounding the cabin.

The small dwelling stood in the centre of an open space that must have been cleared at some time. Maybe an old hunter's cabin, Stafford guessed, or maybe built by an early pioneer wary of the Shoshone. But it looked empty now. There was no sign of life and at this time of the day unless the occupant was sick or wounded he'd have been out of his bunk.

No point in taking chances, though. Stafford held his Colt at arm's length, cocked and ready to fire. Slowly he crossed the open area, his eyes scanning the cabin before him. He reached the door, took a deep breath, turned the roughly carved handle and kicked the door open, rushing in, crouched low.

Nothing stirred. The cabin was one large room. He stared hard at the fall of material over to his right. Somebody behind there, waiting? For a second he thought of firing through the cloth, but realized that would scare Victoria. Not trying to disguise the sound of his boots and spurs he strode across the room and tore the cloth aside.

Only a large empty bunk! His muscles relaxed but then he frowned. For a cabin in the wild the bunk sure was fancy. Cotton sheets, slips covering soft-looking pillows, a finely stitched cover across woollen blankets. He turned and went back to the door.

'OK. C'mon ahead!'

He slid his Colt back into its holster and waited at the door until Victoria appeared through the trees, the dog at her side. She stopped halfway across the open area, and bent slightly to give an order to the animal. Ruff immediately sank to the ground, his head resting on extended paws.

When they were both inside the cabin Stafford pointed across to the bunk. 'Did you see what we got here?'

Victoria shook her head. 'I only saw the English riding crop, then Ruff found me and I rode back to you.'

She walked across the cabin to gaze for a few moments down at the bedding, before letting out a long sigh. 'Oh, Lucy! What were you thinking of?'

Stafford walked across to the rough table and picked up the riding crop. It was roughly the same length as the one Victoria carried. Unlike hers with its silver head, this one had a bone handle, carved in the shape of a bird's beak.

'You sure this belonged to the Andrews gal?'

Victoria nodded. 'I'm sure. I think an Englishman gave it to her a couple of years ago. We rode together when she was at the schoolhouse. She carried it for a while but then it disappeared.'

Stafford remembered Mrs Andrews's remarks about her making her daughter throw away the presents from the Englishman. Lucy had obviously hidden the crop away in this cabin. One big question had to be answered. Who was Lucy meeting in this cabin? He thought for a moment. Frank Brand was a candidate.

He turned slowly in the middle of the room. The cabin was as rough as it must have been the day it was built. An old pot-bellied stove stood in the corner, its blackened pipe leading to a hacked-out hole in the roof. Tufts of bunch and buffalo grass and clods of soil prevented rain from entering the cabin. Alongside the stove a length of timber stood out from the wall of the cabin, preventing Stafford from seeing into the corner. He stepped forward to take a better look. Hanging from a wooden peg was a grey trail jacket. One of its buttons was missing.

'We just struck gold!'

He pulled from the pocket of his own jacket the button he'd found in the hotel room he'd taken at the Majestic. He held out the button to a puzzled-looking Victoria. Then he realized she knew nothing about the jacket. He'd explain later. He turned back to the jacket and plunged his hand into its pockets one by one. Maybe there was something to identify the owner. All the pockets appeared empty but then his hand closed over a scrap of paper, and he turned back to Victoria. He was holding up the paper when the noise of loud barking reached them.

'There's someone outside!' Victoria exclaimed.

Stafford's hand dropped to the butt of his Colt. 'Stay here,' he ordered.

He moved quickly to the door, pulling it open slowly before stepping outside quickly to scan the ground ahead. The dog was standing quite still, his head pointing towards the trees. Stafford brought up his Colt to aim at the shadowy figure he saw moving steadily towards him.

'Hold it right there! You move closer, an' I shoot!'

The figure stopped dead. 'Mr Stafford? Is that you?'

The voice was that of a woman. What the hell was going on here?

He lowered his Colt as he heard Victoria step from the cabin behind him. 'That's Amy's voice,' she exclaimed.

'You certain?'

'Yes, I'm sure.'

'OK, Miss Amy,' he called. 'C'mon ahead.'

They stood there as Amy Brand emerged from the trees. She was white-faced as if the threat of Stafford shooting had caused her alarm. Victoria stepped past Stafford as Amy Brand reached them. She took the younger woman's hands in her own.

'What are you doing here, Amy? How did you find us?'

'Mr Galton explained where you were,' she said. 'I had to find Mr Stafford before it was too late.'

Stafford reholstered his Colt. 'You wanna explain that, Miss Amy?'

'Jack Hardman and some of his men are

planning to break Frank out of jail,' she said, her voice near to breaking. 'I heard them mention Mr Worley's name as well.'

Stafford thought fast. Hardman threatening to bust out young Brand meant that whatever was going on in Storm was falling apart. This was the result he'd been hoping for when he had young Brand jailed. But Amy Brand's mention of Worley's name made him uneasy Hardman might be reckoning on another payout if he put Tom out of the way.

He became aware that Amy Brand was gazing up at him, tears in her eyes. 'I fear for Mr Worley's life, Mr Stafford,' she said. 'When he's found innocent of that dreadful killing we intend to be married.'

CHAPTER NINE

'Hardman would never be that crazy!' Mackay shouted, although Stafford was only the other side of his desk. The sheriff threw down the pen he'd been writing with in a large leather-bound book. The pen bounced on the surface of the desk and fell to the floor.

'Who fed you that horseshit?' Mackay said, his body rigid, leaning across the desk towards Stafford.

'Amy Brand,' said Stafford evenly 'She overheard him talking with some of his men out at the Double B.'

Mackay's eyes widened with surprise. He fell back in his chair, mixed emotions chasing across his face. 'Goddamnit, Stafford!' he exploded. 'Storm Creek was a peaceful town until you rode in.'

A young girl with her throat cut and attacks on homesteads didn't rate as peaceful in his book, but it wasn't the time to say it, Stafford decided. He kept his mouth shut, sitting relaxed in his chair, waiting for

Mackay's next move.

The sheriff appeared to calm down, his brow furrowing. 'You reckon Hardman really means to bust out Brand?'

Stafford nodded. 'I reckon so. Amy Brand told me enough to convince me. If I know Hardman he'll come in with a few of his men when the town's quiet. He'll be hopin' that you'll do most things to avoid a gunfight an' let Brand go.' He glanced out of the window at a wagon passing down Main Street. 'Today's a trading day. He'll know the wagons will be gone by noon, an' the town'll be quiet. He'll come in then, I reckon.'

Mackay's mouth turned down. 'I hear Hardman's fast.'

Faster than you can even imagine, Stafford thought, but again there was nothing to gain by saying so. He became aware that Mackay was looking past him, staring into nowhere.

Then Mackay gave a short barking laugh. 'I've seen this comin',' he said finally Mackay shook his head, refocusing on Stafford. 'I ain't blamin' you. I shoulda done somethin' about Hardman an' his gunslingers afore now.'

'You got anyone mebbe stand with you?' Stafford asked.

Mackay shrugged. 'You seen Charlie, my deputy. He's got one eye and six brats. I ain't even gonna ask him. I'll post him to the north. He can tell me when Hardman's comin' in.'

'Any o' the townsfolk?'

Mackay shook his head. 'Ten years ago, there'd have been half a dozen, but times change. Ribbon clerks, corn merchants, blacksmiths, they're the sorta fellers you now get in a town like this. They're good men, but they couldn't handle this.'

'Then I guess it'll just be the two of us,' Stafford said.

'Now listen–' Mackay began but broke off as the street door opened. Harry Galton stepped into the office. 'Mrs Ross tol' me that Hardman's comin' in with his trail-trash.' He looked at Stafford. 'She got that right?'

'Hardman's gonna try an' bust out young Brand.'

Galton nodded. 'Guessed that was it. You standin' with Mr Mackay?'

'Yeah, seems the right thing to do.'

'Let me know when you need me.'

'Mr Galton!' Mackay exclaimed. 'You don't even wear a gun.'

Galton looked at him, a faint smile on his face. 'I'll be armed, Mr Mackay.' Without a further word he turned and left the office.

There was silence in the office for a few moments before Mackay spoke.

'Seems I got more support in this town than I thought,' he said slowly, looking at the door that Galton had closed behind him.

Stafford got to his feet. 'I gotta talk with Mrs Morgan afore she leaves Widow Brown's place. You'd best get Charlie lookin' to the north. An' I'm gonna need more slugs for my Colt, an' a coupla Winchesters.'

Stafford raised a finger to an eyebrow in a mock salute as Mackay got up from his seat. 'I'll be hereabouts at noon,' he said.

Stafford reached Widow Brown's clapboard in time to see Daisy Morgan climbing into the buckboard seat alongside Theo Morgan.

'Good day, Mrs Morgan,' Stafford said before turning to the ex-soldier. 'I guess you finished fendin' for yourself, Theo.'

Morgan showed a mouthful of large teeth between his black moustaches and beard. 'That's 'bout it, Cap'n.' Morgan looked at his wife. 'I swear Mrs Morgan's lookin' ten years younger.'

Daisy Morgan beamed at her husband. And it was true, Stafford thought, looking at her face. She did look much better after her break from the exhausting work needed to keep the homestead running. Maybe it had been necessary to have her help lure the Double B no-goods into a trap, but it was good that she'd gained something from the plan.

'That she is,' Stafford said, replying to Morgan. 'You got a few moments? I wanna ask you somethin'.'

'Ask away, Cap'n.'

'No need to bother Mrs Morgan with this, Theo. But I've a question for Mrs Morgan as well, afore you leave town.'

Morgan locked the wheels of the buckboard before handing the reins to his wife. He stepped down into the street and followed Stafford the few paces that took them out of Mrs Morgan's hearing. Keeping his voice low, Stafford spoke for several minutes to Morgan. When he'd finished he looked enquiringly at Morgan.

'What you reckon, Theo?'

'Yeah, I got it, Cap'n. Reckon there's gonna be no problem with that.'

Satisfied, Stafford turned back to the buckboard. Mrs Morgan had her head turned in Stafford's direction. The expression on her face plainly showed that she was a little apprehensive.

He smiled reassuringly 'Don't you worry 'bout this, Mrs Morgan, but I need to know what you fed me when you were nursin' me at Joe Bagley's place.'

Stafford's question seemed to catch Daisy Morgan off balance. Her anxious frown deepened. 'You ain't mad at me, Mr Stafford?'

'No, ma'am, I'm not. I'm thinkin' of that first day I was up an' about. You'd already left, I recall. I just remember feelin' better than I should for a feller who'd been kicked by no-goods. I'm guessin' at somethin', that's all.'

Daisy Morgan appeared to take a deep breath. 'You was hurtin' bad, Mr Stafford. So I gave you laudanum, keep you quiet an' peaceful.' She looked at him anxiously. 'Joe Bagley said you had to get back on your feet real fast. The men needed you, he said.'

'You did right, Mrs Morgan, an' I'm mighty grateful.' He played what he hoped was a winning card. 'I s'pose Doc Mayerling gave you the opium,' he said casually

Daisy Morgan shook her head. 'The doctor's mighty careful,' she said. 'If he reckons anyone needs it, he brings it himself.' She hesitated as if unsure how Stafford would react to her words. 'I buy mine from Mr Chang at the eating-house.'

Stafford laid a hand on her arm. 'Mrs Morgan, you've been a great help. Now Mr Morgan's got a coupla small errands, but then you just get back an' enjoy your home. Those no-goods at the Double B are gonna think twice afore they make trouble agin.'

Daisy Morgan's face split into a big smile. She must have been a real pretty girl when Morgan married her, Stafford decided.

'You've been real kind, Cap'n Stafford,' she said.

He stood back as the buckboard rolled forward, his hand raised in farewell. Daisy Morgan staying in the rooming-house had paid off in more ways than he'd expected. He knew he might not have thought about her nursing had he not had to settle with Widow Brown.

As he knocked on the door of the clap-board Stafford considered his next move. So along with good grub and coffee Chang was also selling opium outside the control of Mayerling. Maybe he'd been selling it to Lucy Andrews. Stafford looked up at the sun. There was time before noon to go and shake some information out of Storm Creek's celestial.

Chang's eating-house was busy when Stafford entered the large room. Some of the men looked up as he crossed to the table in a corner. The red-haired man who owned Storm's newspaper looked hard at him for a few moments, but must have seen something in Stafford's face, as he ducked his head and turned back to his companions. Chang appeared in front of Stafford's table.

'Just coffee,' Stafford said.

A few moments later the coffee was put before him. Stafford took a sip. It was good coffee, strong and black. Now that he had chance to sit and turn over his thoughts he considered what was likely to happen when Hardman came into town. Something must be going badly wrong for him to think of breaking Frank Brand out of jail.

Was Frank Brand the killer of Lucy Andrews? Had young Brand been meeting up with Lucy Andrews at the cabin in the wood? Stafford suddenly thought of the trail jacket he'd found. He should have brought it back to town. He'd got the scrap of paper from the pocket but it wasn't enough. Had he brought the jacket into Storm, Mackay could have made Brand try it on for size. He turned the thought over. Maybe that's what Hardman was about. Was Elisha Brand worried that his only son was about to break down and confess to the killing? His thoughts were interrupted by Chang appearing in front of his table.

'All finished now, Mr Stafford.'

Stafford looked around the room, seeing it was empty. He laid a coin on the table and stood up as if preparing to leave. Then his hand shot out to grasp the Chinaman by his upper arm. Ignoring Chang's protests he herded him across to the back room where the food was prepared. He looked inside. The room was empty.

He turned and marched the protesting Chang across the room to the nearest table, and forced him down in a chair. 'You're sellin' opium, Chang. I wanna hear about your customers.'

Chang began to shake his head in denial. Stafford drew his Colt, and looked around. 'That fancy gewgaw,' – he pointed with the barrel of his sidearm to a richly painted vase standing on a high shelf – 'You brought it from the old country?'

Chang nodded furiously 'Very honourable,' he said. 'From my ancestors.'

Stafford nodded. 'I'm gonna count to three, Chang. You tell me 'bout sellin' opium to Lucy Andrews, or you're gonna part company with your ancestors.'

'No! No! I not sell opium to Miss Lucy!'

'One,' Stafford said, cocking his sidearm.

'I swear, I swear.'

'Two.'

Chang raised himself from his chair, his hands fluttering weakly towards the rigid arm of Stafford who looked directly at the vase. His trigger finger began to tighten.

'I sell it to Mr Brand!' Chang shouted.

Stafford lowered his arm, remembering Hardman's mention of the old rancher being sick. Brand hadn't looked healthy at the town's party, he recalled.

'Elisha Brand?'

Chang shook his head vigorously, relief showing in his face. 'No, not Mr Elisha. I sell it to Mr Frank! I think he give it to Miss Lucy.'

Stafford and Mackay were sitting silently in the sheriff's office when the door was flung open and Charlie, the deputy burst in. 'They're on their way sheriff! I seen 'em soon as they came over the hill.'

'How many you see, Charlie?' Mackay asked.

'Five, I reckon.' He hesitated, his teeth

snagging his lip. 'Mr Mackay, I'm your deputy an'–'

'No, Charlie,' Mackay said quickly. 'You ain't signed up for this sorta happenin'.' He glanced at Stafford. 'Anyways, I got Mr Stafford an' Mr Galton badged up. You go an' tell Mr Galton it's time. Then get yourself home.'

Charlie stood still for a moment. Then he turned on heel and went out into the street. Mackay tugged at an earlobe.

'Folks sure can be surprisin',' he said slowly.

Stafford looked up from pushing extra ammunition for his Colt into his belt. Beside him open boxes of ammunition stood on the corner of Mackay's desk.

'It ain't too late,' he said. 'Let Brand and Tom Worley go, an' you solve everythin'. Hardman backs off. Me an' Worley leave town. Coupla months the townsfolk will be wonderin' why we all got het up.'

Mackay snorted. 'Not in my town! Sure, we need more law 'round these parts. An' a year or two we'll see it. But 'til then it's just me.' He bit hard into his lip. 'If it means I gotta face Hardman, then that's the hand I been dealt an' I'm gonna play it.'

Stafford got to his feet. He hoped his face

140

didn't give Mackay any idea of how he was feeling. He was remembering something old Amos Jackson had said to him only a couple of weeks before Amos had died down in Kansas.

'Make sure you don't stay in this game too long, Luke,' Amos had said. 'It ain't just a question of who's the fastest with a gun. This life's like gambling. Sooner or later the cards are gonna turn agin you. Make sure you get out before they do.'

Stafford filled his lungs with air. He looked directly at Mackay. 'OK, Sheriff. Let's go an' deal with these no-goods.'

The two men stepped out onto the boardwalk. As if waiting for his cue, Galton appeared at the entrance to his store. He crossed the boardwalk on his side, stepped down to the hardpack of Main Street, and crossed to meet Stafford and Mackay as they reached the middle of the street.

Galton was still wearing the trousers of his city suit, Stafford saw, but over the vest he normally wore he had on a short leather jacket, unbuttoned, that fell only as far as his waist. There was no sign of a sidearm.

Not a man or woman was to be seen in Main Street. The townsfolk appeared to have had news of what was about to happen. With the trading over for the day they had disappeared behind closed doors. Stafford turned and looked beyond the roofs of the three two-storey buildings that lined Main Street among the other stores. The sun would be behind them, in the faces of Hardman and his men as they came into town.

'They're here,' barked Mackay

The three men separated, stringing themselves across the street to avoid giving a bunched-up target to Hardman and his men. Stafford stood in the middle of the street staring at the five men who rode towards them. Hardman would try and talk, he guessed. He wouldn't have his men try and ride them down.

Sure enough, Hardman pointed towards the hitching rail in front of the dry goods store, and the five turned the heads of their mounts. A few moments later, having hitched up their horses, they began to walk steadily towards Stafford and the other two.

Stafford stood easy his hands loosely held down by his sides. From the corners of his eyes, he could see first Mackay, and then Galton. Both men were taut, their heads still, their stares unwavering. Hardman reached maybe thirty feet from the line of three men.

'Mighta known you'd be in this, Luke,' Hardman said.

'Tol' you once, Jack. Guess you weren't listenin'.'

Stafford allowed his gaze to shift along the line of Hardman's men. The gunman at the end, sporting a bright red neckerchief, looked as taut as a Comanche bowstring. His curled fingers were inches away from the butt of his sidearm.

'You pull your gun in this street, Hardman, you're gonna be joinin' Frank Brand,' Mackay called.

Hardman's mouth pulled back, the smile not reaching his eyes. He looked at the three men in turn. His gazed lingered on Harry Galton, who stood at an angle to the Double B men. Hardman's frown deepened.

'You're that picture-makin' feller, ain't you? What the hell you doin' out here?'

'Aw fer Chris'sakes!' red neckerchief shouted. 'Quit all this talkin'!'

His hand dropped to his sidearm. His fingers had barely started to grasp the butt when metal flashed across the street. For an instant he was as rigid as a toy doll held taut by strings. His hand fluttered towards the short knife protruding from his throat. Blood spurted as he pitched forward face

143

first into the dirt, and lay still.

'Jesus Christ!'

The gunman on Hardman's right was slack jawed, his hand lifting away from the butt of his Colt. Stafford fought hard to control his own expression. He hadn't been aware that Galton had even moved. How the hell had he got the knife or whatever it was to reach across the street? But now was the time to grab the advantage.

'One down, Jack,' Stafford said. 'You ain't forgettin' we usedta try an' not be out-numbered?'

'Four of us, Luke. Three o' you.'

'Look up at the roofs. Them sod-busters you stirred up are feelin' real ornery.'

Hardman didn't take his eyes off Stafford. A slow smile appeared on his face. 'You usedta be a lousy poker player, Luke. Always lost the pot on a crazy bluff.'

For a second or two Stafford was silent. Then slowly he began to raise his right hand away from his side until it was well clear of the butt of his Colt. Call my bluff, he was telling Hardman. The gunman to the right of Hardman decided to call it. His gun was half-way out of his holster when the Winchester slug fired from the top of the Majestic slammed into his chest sending him hurling

144

back. He attempted one blood-choked cry, his feet drumming in the dirt for a moment or two, and then he was suddenly still. Stafford waited, his hand now back close to the butt of his Colt. If Hardman was going to try anything this was the moment.

Hardman appeared to be weighing the odds, glancing between the three men who stood facing him. Then, without a word, he slowly turned and began to walk back to his horse. His two men were left standing, their faces showing their confusion.

'You got five minutes to get outa town,' Mackay roared. He pointed in turn to the two bodies in the dirt. 'An' take this trail-trash with you!'

'Not afore I get what's mine,' Galton called.

He strode across the street to the body of the gunman whom he had felled. With a quick jerk he pulled out the knife and with a couple of sweeps wiped off the blood on the man's clothes.

'I'm sure glad you didn't miss with that knife,' said Mackay soberly, as the three watched Hardman's men dragging away the bodies.

Wordlessly, Galton pushed back the flap of his leather jacket. In a belt across his body, an inch or two above his waist nestled half a dozen similar short knives.

'What the hell you got there?' Mackay asked.

'*Kozuka*,' Galton said.

Stafford exchanged puzzled looks with Mackay. 'No, I ain't got a notion of what he's talkin' 'bout either,' he said. 'Mebbe Hardman should've brought all his no-goods into town!' Stafford's grin faded, and he frowned. 'Yeah, an' why didn't he?'

CHAPTER TEN

'Tom, I hope this place ain't sendin' you a mite crazy,' Stafford said.

He stared down at the slip of paper Worley had thrust in his hand through the bars. He read the note again to make sure he'd understood Worley's instructions. 'You want me to take this to the livery an' Fellowes is to place this order with money you've got in the bank?'

'That's it, Luke. No use asking Josh Andrews. He'll just ignore it.'

'You mind tellin' me what you're up to?'

Worley shook his head. 'Not yet, Luke. I'm not certain I've understood the law.'

'Yet you're gonna gamble this money?'

Worley's mouth pulled up. 'In a month maybe I'll not be worrying about money.'

Stafford looked hard at his friend. 'Now don't you get thinkin' like that. I'm gonna get you outa here.' He looked along the passageway as Mackay appeared with a bunch of keys and began to unlock Brand's cell.

'OK, Mr Mackay, I'm ready,' Stafford told

147

the sheriff.

He thrust his hand through the bar and gripped Worley's arm. 'The sheriff's doin' this only 'cos o' yesterday's stand-off with Hardman,' he said. 'But it's a chance to get him thinkin'. Keep your head up, Tom.'

He turned away and followed Brand and Mackay into the office.

'Sit there, Brand,' Mackay ordered. 'We got some questions.'

Brand fell, rather than sat, on the chair Mackay had pushed into the centre of the room. Stafford leaned against the wall, his eyes on Brand while Mackay crossed the office to lock the street door. He gave a brief nod in Stafford's direction.

'Get your head up, Brand. I wanna see your face.' Stafford barked.

Slowly, the young man raised his head, looking first at the sheriff and then at Stafford. The time in jail had marked him, Stafford saw. The freshness of the young man he'd first seen on his way into Storm had gone. His eyes had hardened and he held Stafford's stare. Brand was going to fight for his life whatever he'd done, Stafford realized. The young man had found strength from somewhere even if it was the courage of desperation.

'I didn't want to do it,' Brand said defiantly. 'He made me.'

'You sayin' your father made you kill that gal?'

'What the hell–?' Brand broke off, a horrified look appearing on his face. 'I'm not talkin' 'bout Lucy Andrews. I'm talkin' 'bout the raid on Morgan's place.'

'Forget that,' Stafford said. 'Hardman's no-goods got what they deserved.'

'How long you been buying opium from Chang?' Mackay asked suddenly.

Brand's head jerked around. 'How d'you know that?'

'I told him,' Stafford said. 'How long?'

Brand's teeth dug into his lower lip. 'Six months, mebbe seven.'

'An' how long were you givin' it to Lucy Andrews?'

Brand half rose from his chair. 'I ain't done no such thing.'

'Sit down!' Mackay roared. He stepped forward, and thrust Brand back into his seat. 'You were carryin' on with that poor gal in secret. Feedin' her opium, gettin' her to go out to that cabin with you. She get uppity with you, Frank? Thought you was playin' for keeps? Was she gonna tell your father, claim she was gonna marry you? A foolish

149

young gal from a store gonna try and claim a slice of the Double B?'

Brand shook his head so hard it seemed to Stafford that he'd throw himself off his chair. 'No! No! I swear you got it wrong, Mr Mackay! What the hell's all this 'bout a cabin? I never took Lucy anywhere. Sure we were friends. She was a friendly gal. But nothin' like that, I swear.'

Mackay looked across at Stafford who gave an almost imperceptible shake of his head. The sheriff grabbed Brand by his arm. 'I ain't finished yet. We're gonna have more questions. You're back in the cage.'

While Mackay dragged Brand out of the office back to his cell Stafford crossed the office and unlocked the door. Young Brand was proving tougher than expected. All Brand had to do, Stafford realized, was to keep on denying everything until Tom Worley came up for trial. Unless Brand's story could be broken Worley would hang. He breathed in deeply. Where the hell was he going from here? He looked up as Mackay entered.

'I ain't sure if he's lyin',' Mackay said.

He walked over to the stove and took down two mugs from the hooks on the wall. He poured coffee and brought the mugs

150

over to the desk. Then he settled himself in his chair, looking thoughtfully at Stafford.

'What you gonna do now?'

Stafford didn't reply immediately. Instead he walked over to the corner of the office and picked up the two Winchester rifles Jenkins and Miller had used on the roof tops the day before. He checked that the long guns had been cleaned before walking over to the gun cabinet and stowing them securely. He then sat down again in front of the desk.

'Brand's fighting for his life. I reckon he'd say anythin' that he thinks would save him. Harry Galton's gone out to the cabin. He's gonna bring back the trail jacket I found. We'll see if it fits Brand.'

Mackay was about to reply when the street door opened. Both men rose to their feet.

'Good mornin', Mrs Ross,' Mackay said. 'A fine day, and now even finer for seeing you.'

Victoria Ross acknowledged the compliment with a brief bow of her head. 'Why thank you, Mr Mackay.'

As she settled her skirts in the chair that Mackay brought forward she exchanged smiles with Stafford, her eyes sparkling with pleasure. But then her expression became serious. She took a scrap of paper from the small bag she was carrying.

'This is the paper I found in the trail jacket out at the cabin,' Stafford explained to Mackay. 'It tells Lucy to go to the room in the Majestic. It's not in Tom Worley's hand. I've checked.'

'Neither is it in Lucy's hand,' Victoria said. 'I've come straight from seeing Mr Andrews in the store.' Seeing Mackay frown she explained further. 'Luke wished to be sure that the note wasn't some sort of prank played by Lucy that went terribly wrong.'

Mackay's frown deepened. 'Where's the note telling Worley to go to the hotel?'

Stafford's mouth twitched. Was Mackay having doubts about Worley's guilt? Maybe when Galton got back with the jacket and they made Frank Brand wear it, Worley's situation might change.

'He saw no reason to keep it, and destroyed it,' Stafford said, answering Mackay. 'He was convinced that it was from Amy Brand.'

Mackay nodded slowly, apparently thinking through what he'd just learned. 'Now just hold on,' he said suddenly. 'OK, mebbe I shoulda checked this beforehand but the answer seemed clear with Worley comin' outa the room with a knife in his hand. That room musta been reserved, or how did

152

Worley know which room to go to?'

'The room was reserved in the name of Amy Brand,' Victoria Ross said quietly.

Mackay, who'd been addressing his remarks to Stafford, spun around in his chair to glare at her across the desk. His good manners flew out of the window.

'How the heck d'you know that?'

'Yesterday evening I went to see Mr Kenney at the Majestic.' Unfazed by Mackay's sudden lack of courtesy, Victoria continued to smile at the sheriff. 'He was good enough to go through all his books and find out how the room had been taken.'

'I asked Mrs Ross to do that,' Stafford explained. 'I reckoned she'd have better luck with Kenney with his little girl attending the schoolhouse.'

Mackay dropped back in his chair, his mouth opening and closing as if struggling to get out his words. He looked first at Stafford and then at Victoria Ross, his face reddening. He threw his hands in the air.

'Ain't that just great! Yesterday I make it through a gunfight as if this town was Abilene,' he barked. 'I got the only son of the most powerful rancher in the territory in my jail. Now I got his daughter reserving the room for a killin'.'

'I didn't say that, Mr Mackay,' Victoria said quickly. 'Mr Kenney said the room was in her name. He couldn't recall Miss Amy arranging it herself. I suspect he knew she'd been meeting Tom Worley there but Mr Kenney was sure it was always Tom who made the arrangements, and only ever in his name.'

Victoria Ross got to her feet. 'Now you must excuse me, gentleman. I have business to attend to.'

The two men stood, as with a swirl of skirts and a faint scent of fresh flowers she left the office, directing one last smile at Stafford as she closed the door. Mackay dropped back to his seat.

'Goddamnit! If only Jamie Brand had lived I reckon none o' this woulda happened. He'd have handled the homesteaders, Elisha woulda never needed Hardman an' his bunch o' no-goods, an' I reckon that poor gal would be alive today.'

'That's a couple times I've heard Jamie Brand's name,' Stafford said.

'A fine man, ten years older than his brother,' Mackay said. 'A mite too fond of the ladies, some folks said. But he never caused trouble. Got hisself killed in a huntin' accident.'

A knock came at the street door before the door was pushed open and a short stocky man stepped into Mackay's office. He wore a smooth grey Prince Albert over a soft white shirt. A heavy gold chain showed across his silk vest. As Mackay got to his feet the newcomer swept off his fashionable hat.

'Good day to you, Mr Mackay.' His voice hinted at origins back East and was well-modulated.

'Good day, Mr Simpson.' Mackay jerked his head in Stafford's direction. 'This tough-lookin' feller here is Mr Luke Stafford. This gentleman, Luke, is Mr Josiah Simpson, lawyer to Elisha Brand.'

'Ah! Mr Stafford. I've heard much about you.'

Stafford nodded, acknowledging Simpson's remarks. He realized this was the lawyer Tom had mentioned on his first day in Storm. Beneath the city manners, Tom had said, Simpson was as dangerous as a rattlesnake.

'What can I do for you?' Mackay asked.

The lawyer reached into an inside pocket of his Prince Albert. With a flourish he laid papers on Mackay's desk.

'You can release Mr Frank,' he said.

In the process of reaching for the papers, Mackay stopped suddenly, his hand six

155

inches above the desk.

'Is this some sort of jest, Mr Simpson?' Stafford said.

'I never jest about the law, Mr Stafford,' Simpson said. 'Yesterday afternoon the men who accompanied Mr Frank to the Morgan homestead swore on oath in front of the Justice of the Peace at South Pass that Mr Frank had no notion of their intentions to attack the Morgan home. He thought they were merely going to speak with Mr Morgan.'

So that's why Hardman brought in less men than expected, Stafford realized. 'You sayin' that aimin' to fire the barn was part of talkin'?' he asked.

'Look at the papers, Mr Mackay. All the men have sworn that the dead man, Cassidy, was an uncontrollable hothead.' He turned with a half smile towards Stafford. 'In any event, the blackguard got what he deserved, do you not agree?'

Mackay looked up from reading the papers Simpson had given him. 'It's all here, Luke, all legal,' he said. 'I gotta do what Miss Morris tells me to.'

'Those men are lyin'!' Stafford exploded.

'Those men are heading for six months breaking rocks in Cheyenne,' said Simpson.

156

'They're not men who willingly go to prison.'

'Unless Elisha Brand paid them well,' said Stafford grimly.

Simpson didn't reply. Instead, he turned to the sheriff. 'Mr Mackay, shall we proceed?'

Mackay, his face expressionless, reached behind his chair for the keys before crossing the office to go through the door to the cages. A few moments later he reappeared accompanied by Frank Brand. Stafford eyed the young man stonily. Tom Worley's chances were becoming slimmer by the minute.

'Come along, Mr Frank,' Simpson said. 'I've a horse waiting for you.'

Brand, moving to the door behind the lawyer, stopped in front of Stafford, looking straight into his eyes. He held Stafford's glare for a few seconds before speaking.

'Since that day my horse broke his leg out on the trail I've been actin' plain stupid. But you're plumb wrong about Lucy Andrews. I ain't done what you're accusin' me of.'

Stafford grunted. 'You're walkin' away from the Morgan raid 'cos you got a smart lawyer. That don't fret me all that much. But I'm tellin' you now, it ain't gonna be Tom Worley who swings for that gal.'

Tom Worley looked up from writing on the paper resting on a square of wood. His inkpot stood on the small stool close to his bunk. Worley looked across to Stafford who stood at the bars.

'My lawyer's skills come in handy at a time like this,' Worley said.

'What's that you're writing, Tom?'

'My will,' said Worley flatly.

'For Chris'sakes! Don't give up, Tom. We still gotta coupla weeks. We ain't done yet.'

Worley shook his head. 'I'm facing facts, Luke. And they're all against me. They have been from the beginning.' His eyes moved away from Stafford for a moment before looking back. 'I know you tried your damnedest and I'm really grateful. But seeing Brand walk away just now means the last chance has gone.'

The knuckles on Stafford's hand around the bar a few inches from his eyes turned white. 'Bagley an' the men ain't gonna think too much of it,' he said sharply, 'you give up fightin'.'

Worley sighed. 'Maybe I been fightin' too long, Luke.' He sat up suddenly, as if he'd remembered something. 'Anyways, I got some good news for the men.' He gestured to the pile of law books on his bunk. 'Their time in the army counts to the five years needed to own their homesteads outright. Only a few more months and they'll be in the clear.' Worley managed a smile. 'Elisha will never forgive me.'

Stafford swore. 'Tom, I was wrong to talk o' the men! You gotta think o' yourself!'

'You mean like you, Luke?' Worley said wryly. 'Going out and facing Hardman and his gunmen?'

'That was–' Stafford stopped suddenly. He loosed his grip on the bar and turned on his heel to head back down the passage.

'Tom!' he shouted over his shoulder. 'We ain't done yet!'

Mackay half rose from his chair as Stafford burst through the door.

'Somethin' wrong back there?'

Stafford looked hard at Mackay. 'Why would Elisha Brand have Hardman try an' break out his son if he'd already paid off the no-goods to swear a bunch o' lies?'

Mackay, a resigned expression on his face, dropped back to his chair.

'Fer Chris'sakes,' he said, his voice loud. 'We been all through this! If Brand killed Lucy Andrews, an' I ain't sayin' he did, he mighta broken down and confessed. Elisha thought it safer to have him outa here.'

159

'All for a few hours? Elisha Brand's smart an' he's gotta smart lawyer.' Stafford's voice had also risen to an angry shout. 'You reckon a man like Elisha is gonna go in for Main Street gunfights?'

The young man who stood at the open door to the street made a sound, shooting nervous looks in the direction of both men as they swung around suddenly aware they were not alone.

'What is it, Tommy?' Mackay asked, his voice softer.

The young man held up the square package in his hands. 'More books for Mr Worley, sir. The stage just got in.

'OK, you tell 'em I'll be along.'

Tommy stepped forward and placed the books on Mackay's desk. Then, with a backward glance at Stafford, he left the office, closing the door carefully as if one of the men might call him back.

Mackay crossed to open the door to the cages. 'More books, Mr Worley,' he called. 'You know what I gotta do.'

Stafford didn't catch Worley's reply but Mackay closed the door and went back behind his desk. From his drawer he pulled out a knife.

'Feller in the next county jail got a pack-

160

age like this,' he said. 'Sheriff gave it to him an' found hisself looking down the barrel of a derringer. Since then we gotta open 'em all.'

Stafford looked at the package without much interest. Worley's address was on the side facing him. He wasn't about to admit it to Worley but maybe books were too late. He watched as Mackay opened the blade and leaned over the package to slice at the wrapping paper, his knife effortlessly cutting through the inked address.

Mackay's head shot up, startled by Stafford's shout.

'What the hell's wrong with you? I tol' you, I gotta do this.'

Stafford was on his feet, his eyes fixed on the parcel. He swung around, snatching up his hat from the table beside the door. Without a word he flung open the door and ran down the steps from the boardwalk into the street.

He could wait for Harry to get back, he told himself, as he stepped out, his spurs jingling, towards Galton's store. He'd be back in an hour. Hell! That would be the longest hour of his life. With luck, Harry would have left his store unlocked.

Stafford reached the sign that claimed

Galton had worked with Mathew Brady 'the famous Civil War photographer'. His hand grabbed the door handle. He turned and pushed. The door opened, and he strode across the room to the cabinet which held the photographs Galton had taken at Smallwood's funeral parlour. He slid the photographs out from the drawer and lined them up on Galton's desk.

He exhaled breath noisily, feeling the tension in his shoulder muscles as he bent to peer closely at each photograph in turn. Galton had done well, he remembered. The slashed throat of Lucy Andrews was in perfect focus. For a moment he stared hard at the terrible wound. After a few moments he stood up and looked across Main Street in the direction of the jailhouse. A grim smile began to show on his weather-beaten face.

CHAPTER ELEVEN

Stafford came back into the Majestic having taken breakfast. There was nothing like a good chunk of honest beef and a couple of eggs to set up a man for the day. He'd considered going to the eating-house at the other end of town, but guessed that Chang's liking for profit would outweigh any bad feelings. He'd guessed right. The celestial had greeted him warmly as if nothing had happened between them, but Stafford had noticed that the painted pot was no longer standing on its high shelf.

'I'll take my key, Mr Kenney,' he said.

The desk clerk nodded towards the corner of the lobby. 'Double B hand to see you, Mr Stafford.'

Stafford turned to see a short wiry man rise from a chair, his hat in his hand. Stafford vaguely recalled seeing him among the group of cowboys in the saloon the day he arrived in Storm.

'Mr Elisha Brand asks if you'd join him in the Nugget. There's coffee an' breakfast if

163

you ain't taken it.'

Stafford remained expressionless. The last time they'd met, Brand was full of threats. Now it sounded as if he was keen to parlay. Why not talk with the rancher? He had some time on his hands. Harry Galton wouldn't be back for a couple of hours, having volunteered to ride out to the cabin and retrieve the trail jacket and the riding crop.

'Tell Mr Brand, I'll be along,' he said.

Half an hour had passed when Stafford pushed through the batwing doors of the saloon. If Brand was keen to talk with him, Stafford reckoned, he would have waited. Sure enough, in the otherwise deserted saloon, Brand was seated at a table over on the right of the saloon. A coffee pot that might have been made of silver stood on the table in front of him. Alongside the pot stood a small jug made of the same metal.

Stafford walked to the table, his boots disturbing the thin layer of sawdust on the floor. He halted at the table, and looked down at Brand who had remained in his seat. There were black shadows beneath the rancher's eyes. The flesh of his face had a faint blue tinge. His hand that rested by his cup and saucer showed a slight tremor.

'Sit down and take coffee, Mr Stafford,'

Brand said. 'George will bring you breakfast if you wish.'

'Coffee's fine.'

Brand looked across the saloon. George, the barkeeper, moved quickly, a china cup and saucer in his hand. He came to the table and poured coffee for Stafford who waved away the proffered jug of cream.

'Thank you, George. That will be all.'

'Yes, Mr Brand.'

Brand watched George return to the bar before turning back to Stafford.

'George came here from New York ten years ago without a dollar in his pocket,' he said. 'I gave him a job at the ranch, and later got him work in Storm. He worked hard, and now he owns all this.' Brand waved a hand to take in the saloon.

'You got me here to talk of your philanthropy?' Stafford said.

An amused glint showed in Brand's eyes. 'An interesting word you've chosen to use, Mr Stafford. I see now that Hardman was right about you. He tells me it took him a year to discover you'd been an officer during the War.' Brand's cup on the table rattled slightly and the rancher moved his hand quickly, in an apparent attempt to hide the tremor.

'That Galton feller,' Brand continued. 'I'm told there's more to him than I guessed. Thought he just took pictures of folks. I've been thinking of asking him out to the Double B. Take some pictures of the Big House an' the family.'

Stafford replaced his cup in its saucer. 'Then your cowboys oughta settle their bills,' he said. He stared hard at the old rancher. 'You gonna tell me what you're really after?'

Brand leaned across the table towards Stafford. His mood appeared to have changed in an instant. His face had become redder and the bluish tinge of his skin had deepened save for thin white lines around his nose.

'I want you to stop taking the part o' those damned nesters. I ain't a mean man, Stafford. I pay for what I want. I got five hundred dollars in my poke. They're yourn if you agree.'

Stafford remained silent. Brand must be desperate if he was spreading his money around like this. Getting his son out of jail would have cost him plenty. The men who'd turned themselves in at South Pass wouldn't have agreed to do so unless they'd been paid handsomely. The shoot-out at Morgan's homestead must have shaken the rancher.

'Keep your money,' Stafford said. 'Those "damned nesters" as you call 'em, were once fine soldiers. They're only askin' for the same chance you gave George.'

Brand slammed his hand down causing the china to rattle and the pot to shift on the surface of the table. 'Goddamnit, Stafford! Those nesters are destroying good grass with their damned ploughs.' Spittle flecked the corner of his lips. 'I don't give a damn if they were good soldiers. This is a war, right here in cattle country, an' in a war good men die.'

'You're fightin' time, Brand. Cattlemen are comin' up from the south, homesteaders comin' west by railroad. Hirin' gunslingers can't stop the clock.'

Brand pulled bluish lips back against his teeth. 'I'll make it a thousand dollars, Stafford. Enough to buy the best lawyers in Cheyenne. They'll hogtie any judge the county puts up. No matter Worley killed that gal, he'll walk outa that jailhouse a free man.'

Stafford stood up and pushed back his chair. 'You're in a barrel o' tar, Brand. You've been in it since you hired Hardman. An' I'm gonna get Tom Worley outa jail without the help o' thousand-dollar lawyers.'

He turned on his heel and strode towards

the door, leaving Brand sitting at the table.

Stafford remembered he'd promised to deliver Tom Worley's note to the livery stable. He reckoned he might just have enough time to talk with Fellowes before Galton returned from searching the cabin. He stepped out along the boardwalk. A young woman in blue cotton wearing a long white apron smiled shyly at him and he touched the brim of his hat and wished her a good day. He felt good. At long last he had a handle on what was going on in Storm Creek. Maybe he should have seen it before. But a lot had been happening, and, he reminded himself, getting shot at tends to divert a man's thoughts.

He turned into the alleyway where the side door of the livery was situated. As he approached the door, two men stepped out of the barn. Both were well dressed in dark-coloured Prince Alberts and grey Stetsons.

'Howdy, Mr Stafford,' said the taller of the two.

'Howdy,' Stafford said. Who were these two men? As far as he was aware he had never laid his eyes on either of them.

'The name's Mason,' the darker of the two said. 'This gentleman is Mr Forrester.'

Stafford nodded in acknowledgement.

Was this just a friendly way of passing the time? If so, he would have to tell them he was in a hurry.

'We're both councilmen for Storm Creek, Mr Stafford. We've heard plenty about you. There's a meeting of the council next month. Would you care to attend?'

'You plannin' to run me outa town?'

Mason's neutral expression didn't alter. 'We'd consider it a real favour if you could be there. Good day, sir.'

The two men moved away, leaving a puzzled Stafford staring after them. Was this something to do with Worley? Maybe the stand-off with Hardman and his gunslingers had caused more concern among the townsfolk than Mackay had realized. And Mason hadn't responded to his half-serious question about being run out of town. What the hell! He had more to concern himself with than a couple of councilmen. He stepped into the barn.

'Mr Fellowes!' Stafford called out.

Over to his right his palomino whinnied at the sound of his voice. Horse must be getting used to him. He snatched a handful of hay from a sack hanging from a hook just inside the door and strolled across to the palomino's stall.

169

'Here y'are,' he said, cupping his hand.

Damp rubbery lips rippled across his hand as the palomino took the hay from his palm. Behind him he heard the uneven step of Fellowes.

'Mornin', Mr Stafford. You keep that fine horse here durin' the winter an' I'll give you a special deal.'

Stafford shook his head. 'I'll be leavin' Storm soon, Mr Fellowes, but thanks anyways.' He reached into his pocket and took out the slip of paper. 'I gotta job for you here from Mr Worley.'

Fellowes held out a grimy hand and took the paper from Stafford. 'I sure hope you're gonna get Mr Worley outa that jail. Folks in town beginnin' to realize he'd never do such a terrible thing.'

'I'm gonna do my best,' Stafford said. He pointed to the note. 'Can you fix that?'

Fellowes read the note, looked up at Stafford, and then looked down at the note once more. 'Am I readin' this right? Ten thousand saplings? Mr Worley wants ten thousand saplings?'

'That's what the note says, Mr Fellowes. Can you get 'em?'

'Sure, I can get 'em.' Again he glanced down at the note. 'Mr Worley's feelin' OK, I hope? Know what I mean? He's feelin' himself?'

'He's fine, Mr Fellowes. An' in an hour or so he's gonna feel a lot better.'

Right on cue a voice sounded down the barn from the door.

'Luke! You in here?'

Against the light streaming in through the door of the barn stood Harry Galton, head thrust forward peering into the shadows where Fellowes and Stafford were standing.

'The bank knows you're comin', Mr Fellowes,' said Stafford, as he turned in Galton's direction. 'I'll be back later.'

'I was told you were here,' Galton said, as Stafford reached him. 'I just got back.'

'An' the jacket an' the crop were gone,' Stafford said.

Galton raised his eyebrows. 'How d'you know that?'

'We'll pick up the photographs an' then we'll see Mackay,' Stafford said.

'Fer Chris'sakes, Stafford,' Mackay exploded, 'a coupla hours ago you were sure it was young Brand who killed Lucy Andrews.'

'Frank Brand couldn't have taken the trail jacket and the English riding crop,' Galton said.

171

'The jacket an' the crop coulda been taken by anyone,' Mackay retorted. 'Some trail-trash comes along, stumbles on the cabin looking for shelter, an' steals anythin' he can sell for whiskey. He's likely in Colorado by now.'

'Jack Hardman killed Lucy Andrews,' Stafford said. 'An' I'm gonna prove it to you.'

'How the hell you gonna do that?'

'Harry's gonna cut your throat!'

Mackay jumped from his chair, his eyes shooting between the two men on the other side of his desk, his hand on the butt of his sidearm. 'What the hell you sayin'?'

Stafford's mouth twitched. 'Not for real, Sheriff. We're just gonna be play-actin'.'

The wary look on Mackay's face remained. 'What you want me to do?'

'Harry, move the sheriff's chair and get behind Mr Mackay.'

Galton was slipping a hand beneath his jacket when Mackay held up his hand. 'Play-actin' or not, you ain't gonna use one of them fancy knives. Here!' He picked up a length of wood he used for drawing lines in his ledger. 'This is gonna have to do.'

Stafford nodded. 'That'll be fine.'

Galton moved behind the desk to shift the

chair from behind Mackay and take his position.

'Now Mr Mackay,' Stafford said, 'I want you to tell me what you feel when Harry cuts your throat.' He waited until Mackay nodded his acknowledgement. 'OK, Harry. You know what I want. Go ahead.'

Stafford was glad Galton hadn't a real knife in his hand, even if he was only play-acting. His order to Galton was barely out of his mouth when the length of wood slid across Mackay's throat.

'What did you feel?' Stafford asked.

'What the hell you think?' Mackay ran his thumb along the line traced by the length of wood.

'OK, remember what you've just done. Now I got some pictures for you to look at.'

'Pictures? What the hell you talkin' about?'

Stafford nodded at Galton who reached inside his jacket. Carefully, Galton pulled a small package from an inside pocket. He stepped to the desk while unfolding the wrapping paper. Then he laid the three photographs side by side on Mackay's desk.

Mackay looked down for a second before looking up again at the two men. His expression dared them to say a word as he reached into a drawer in the desk and took out a pair of spectacles. He settled the spectacles on his nose and bent to peer at the photographs in turn for several moments.

'I should run Smallwood outa town,' Mackay muttered, while continuing to examine the photographs.

Galton opened his mouth to speak, but Stafford quickly held up his hand. If this was going to work Mackay had to see it for himself. He watched closely as Mackay moved one of the photographs before putting his thumb to his throat.

'Fer Chris'sakes!' Mackay suddenly shouted.

Stafford let his breath out with a rush of relief, as Mackay stood up and faced him.

'I'm gonna be straight,' Mackay said. 'I see what you're aimin' at, but I ain't sure the judge will pay much attention to these pictures.'

Mackay turned to retrieve his chair, waiting for Galton to move back alongside Stafford, before sitting down. He stared unseeing over Stafford's shoulder for several moments.

'You show those pictures to the judge an' you're gonna have a place in this territory's law-making history,' Stafford said.

Mackay shifted his focus to glare at

Stafford. 'Yeah, an' if he thinks they don't prove nothin' he's gonna kick me all the way to Cheyenne.'

'D'you now think it's possible Hardman killed the girl?' Galton asked.

The sheriff took his time replying. 'If he comes into town I'm gonna put him in a cage an' ask him questions,' he said finally. 'But them pictures ain't enough for a judge an' jury to be sure he killed her.'

'D'you think Hardman coulda moved the stuff from the cabin?'

The sheriff nodded. 'The cabin hidden like you said it ain't likely that some trail-trash took 'em,' he admitted.

'S'posin' I go out an' search Hardman's place at the Double B?' Galton said.

'Harry, that's a crazy notion!' Stafford exclaimed.

'Mr Galton, I ain't doubtin' you're a man of courage,' Mackay said. 'I seen what you did the other day. But Mr Stafford's right: Hardman's tough an' he's got men out there. That's just askin' for a fast ride to Boot Hill.'

Galton looked at Stafford. 'I got an idea, Luke. But we're gonna need Mrs Ross's help.'

'Classes should be finished now,' Stafford

175

told Galton, as they reached the school-house door. He raised his hand to knock but held it in mid-air as he turned to Galton.

'We can think o' somethin' else, Harry. I ain't gonna think less o' you we change our plans.'

In reply Galton raised his own hand and knocked on the door. Stafford pushed open the door, hearing Victoria's voice. As he'd guessed, the children had already left. The room was empty save for Victoria who sat at her table a few feet from her piano.

'Luke! Harry! This is a pleasant surprise.'

She smiled warmly as she stood up behind the table. For a moment Stafford wished that he was here to escort her home, or with a buckboard standing outside to take her for a drive into the country around the town. Maybe even a picnic basket would be in the buggy. He hoped the time would come before he left Storm Creek. But not yet, he told himself, not yet.

'How is Tom?' she asked, her expression becoming anxious.

'He's fine, Victoria. We're gonna get him outa that jail real soon.'

Her eyes widened with pleasure. 'You mean that? Oh, Luke, that would be wonderful.'

'There's somethin' we have to do first,

that's all,' he said slowly.

There's no real risk to Miss Amy, he reminded himself not for the first time since Galton had suggested a plan. He had every right to ask this of her, if it meant that Tom Worley could finally walk out of that jail a free man.

'We need help from Miss Amy. Harry can explain.'

'Anything, Luke,' she said, turning to Galton. 'And I know I can speak for Amy.'

'Elisha Brand has mentioned before that he'd like me to go out to the Double B and take photographs,' Galton said. 'Now I want you to tell Miss Amy that I'll come out and make pictures of her and the family.'

Victoria looked at both men in turn, her eyes asking the question before she spoke. 'That's too simple. What is it you really want?'

Stafford laid his hand on her arm. 'When Harry is photographing Miss Amy he's going to grab the chance to slip away and search Jack Hardman's quarters.'

Her face paled. 'Why? What does Hardman have?'

'Hardman killed Lucy Andrews, Victoria. The jacket and crop have gone from the cabin, an' we reckon Hardman has them.

Finding them will clear Tom.'

Victoria shook her head vigorously. 'It's too risky. If you told Amy what Harry was about she'd panic. And if you don't tell her, then Harry will not be able to slip away.' Her mouth set in a firm line, a determined expression showing on her face. 'I'm Amy's close friend. I'll accompany Harry and he can take photographs of us together. I shall amuse Amy while Harry gets his chance.'

'No!' Stafford exploded. 'It's too dangerous!'

'Then you can't risk Amy,' Victoria retorted. She reached out and placed a hand on Stafford's arm. 'We shall be quite safe. You and Harry have risked your lives for Tom. Amy is to be Tom's wife. Please let me help in this small way.'

Stafford looked at Galton. 'What d'you reckon?'

'I'll photograph the ladies first, search Hardman's quarters, and then pretend a wet plate needs fixin' and I need to return to Storm for a while.' Galton looked at Victoria. 'Everyone dresses in their best for a photograph. Ask Miss Amy to do the same.' He thought for a moment. 'We'll leave town an hour after sun-up. Luke, stay away. Everything must look normal.'

Stafford nodded his agreement. Aware that he was stepping beyond what was proper, and not caring, Stafford reached out and took Victoria's hand. 'One more day, and all this terrible business will be over,' he said, knowing he would not rest a moment until she was safely back in town.

CHAPTER TWELVE

'Luke! What the hell d'you think you're doing?'

Tom Worley's face was white with anger. His face was only a few inches from Stafford, his hands at shoulder level gripping the bars.

'How did you hear?' Stafford asked roughly.

'The sheriff told me.'

'Mackay should keep his mouth shut.' His lower lip curled back over his teeth. 'It's gonna be OK, Tom,' he said.

'No, it's not!' Worley shouted. 'You're risking their lives for nothing!'

'Harry finds that jacket and crop, an' you'll be walkin' outa here.'

Worley stepped back from the bars, resignation showing on his face, as he slumped, head down, on his bunk. Stafford stood at the bars, cursing himself for not telling Mackay to keep his mouth shut.

Worley raised his head. 'Don't you see, Luke? Hardman having the jacket and crop would prove nothing. S'pose he admits to carrying on with Lucy. Where does that leave me?'

'It leaves you a free man.' Stafford retorted. 'Listen, Tom. I know damned well Hardman killed that gal. Those pictures of Harry's are good enough for me.' He breathed in violently, his nostrils flaring. 'I don't give a damn who killed that gal. An' I don't give a damn if Hardman swings for her or walks away. I ain't aimin' to prove to a judge that he killed her. But I put enough doubt in the judge's mind an' you're gonna walk away from all this.' He gripped the bars, his voice rough. 'The ladies will be fine. Harry's a tough son of a gun.'

Worley nodded slowly, managing a weak smile. 'Almost as tough as you, Luke,' he said. He reached across his bunk. 'Anyways, I've good news for Joe Bagley and the men. Come back when the ladies return and I'll explain it to you. And please check if Fellowes has arranged those saplings.'

'I'll do that,' Stafford said more calmly. 'Harry should be back at noon.'

He went down the passageway into Mackay's office. The sheriff looked up as Stafford came through the door. 'I heard the shoutin',' he said. 'Mr Worley was really

181

down this morning. I thought that stuff about Hardman would cheer him up.'

Stafford shrugged. 'I'll be back when Harry Galton returns.'

He went out into Main Street. He wondered for an instant how the town could appear at ease with itself. Folks were going about their business, young women wearing brightly coloured cotton skirts and woollen jackets moved from store to store with their baskets of vegetables and eggs. Men in coveralls and aprons were around the stores. A short skinny man wearing a dusty city suit and a grey derby hat carried a carpet bag in which, Stafford guessed, were his samples.

'So damned normal,' Stafford said aloud.

His words prompted a well-dressed woman accompanied by her maid to jerk her head in his direction. He touched the brim of his hat in unspoken apology, and stepped down to the street.

Had he gone too far this time? Was Tom Worley correct saying that he'd put Brand's daughter and Victoria into danger? He knew he'd never forgive himself if they suffered injury. But surely out at the Double B they'd be safe. Elisha Brand would be around and there'd be some of his cowboys. Hardman was smart. He wasn't likely to cause trouble that would get him fired, and he'd have no notion that he was suspected of killing Lucy Andrews.

'Hey, mister!'

The warning shout broke into his thoughts. Stafford jumped aside, clearing the wagon that had missed him by only a couple of feet. What the hell did he think he was about? He blotted the mental picture of Victoria from his mind as he shouted his apology, but doubted if the wagon driver heard him. Worley's words came back to him. He was tough? Today he wasn't tough enough to cross Main Street safely.

He pushed open the side door to the livery. The morning sun angled through the high double doors. How many days ago was it that he and Victoria had walked their horses through those doors?

'Mornin', Mr Stafford,' Fellowes greeted him, as Stafford walked down the barn. 'I placed that order for the saplings. Mebbe take a few weeks but they'll be here.'

'Thanks, Mr Fellowes. That's all I needed.'

He turned, glancing in the direction of his palomino, and stopped suddenly. The saddle over the door of the next stall was partly in shadow and Stafford stepped across the barn to take a better look.

'This Frank Brand's rig?'

'Sure is,' replied Fellowes. 'He's damned lucky to keep it. Some homesteader brought it in a week back.'

Stafford frowned. 'A good saddle like that, hasn't he been in for it?'

'Oh, sure. That's his new mount he bought coupla days ago.'

'So why's he keeping it here, an' not at the Double B?'

Fellowes hesitated. 'I ain't s'posed to say.' His foot scraped through the straw on the floor of the barn, his head down. Stafford guessed that the liveryman was fighting with his conscience. Frank Brand must have paid him to keep quiet.

'I ain't gonna say a word, Mr Fellowes,' Stafford said softly. 'An' it might help Mr Worley.'

Fellowes looked up. 'Mr Frank's quittin' Storm,' he said. 'Tol' me that he'd had enough.'

'You know where he is?'

Fellowes nodded. 'He's gone to see that fancy lawyer o' his, Mr Simpson. He's got his place coupla stores down from the Frenchie's dry goods.' The liveryman was staring at the retreating figure of Stafford by the time he'd finished speaking.

184

Stafford pushed through the door with its fancy black lettering announcing the office of 'Josiah Simpson, Attorney at Law'. A frail bespectacled man looked up as Stafford entered the office.

'Frank Brand here?'

The little man nodded, his Adam's apple bobbling in his throat. He waved a hand, showing ink-stained fingers, in the direction of a door at the rear of the room.

'That's correct, sir. He's with Mr Simpson. May I ask your business?'

Stafford kept on going, heading for the door indicated by the clerk.

'Sir, I must say–' the little man was heard to protest, his words being cut off by Stafford closing the door behind him as he stepped in to face Simpson and Brand. Both men looked up from their chairs either side of the desk. Frank Brand's face showed surprise at Stafford's sudden entrance. Simpson appeared to maintain his composure.

'If we have business, Mr Stafford, I will see you shortly,' the lawyer said.

'We got nothing to talk about,' Stafford said. 'I'm here to talk with this young feller.'

'Then you must–'

'Mr Simpson, why don't you stroll over to

Chang's an' get yourself some coffee?' Stafford jabbed a thumb over his shoulder before his hand dropped to the butt of his Colt. 'An' take your clerk with you. I get real ornery 'round flappin' ears!'

Simpson stood up. For a few moments he shuffled papers on his desk, his face red. 'We'll finish up later, Mr Frank,' he said. Avoiding Stafford's cold stare, he stepped around the desk and quickly left the room.

Frank Brand was expressionless, looking up at Stafford, apparently waiting calmly to see what this was about. Stafford perched himself on the corner of a nearby table and looked down at the young man.

'I hear you're quittin' the Double B,' Stafford said.

Brand nodded. 'You heard right,' he said evenly. 'Gonna make a clean break, start over someplace else.'

Stafford looked at the young man intently. There was no doubt about it. Whether it was the spell in jail or something else, Frank Brand had changed from the anxious, panicky young man who had tried to steal his palomino. Brand sat relaxed in his chair, quiet determination showing in his eyes. The immature defiance Stafford had observed previously had disappeared.

186

'You sure you're doin' right?' Stafford said. 'Miss Amy cain't run a ranch.' Neither could Tom Worley, he reminded himself. 'Your pa's sick an' he's gonna need your help. You runnin' away ain't doin' nobody any favours.'

'Why should you care what I do?'

Stafford thought for a moment. A picture of a tall young Swede flashed through his mind and he pushed it away. He cursed inwardly. Maybe if he'd asked a couple of more questions a couple of days before he'd have saved lots of folks a heap of trouble.

'That time me an' the sheriff were asking you questions – you remember that?'

'Sure,' Brand said, a puzzled frown appearing on his face.

'You said that you'd been made to take part in the raid on the Morgan homestead.'

Brand's mouth set, and he looked away, avoiding Stafford's eyes.

'Yeah, I said that. I shoulda got out afore then.'

'I thought you were talkin' 'bout your pa,' Stafford said.

Brand's head jerked around. 'That wasn't Pa! He's a hard man, but he wouldn't do that!'

'Take it easy,' Stafford said. 'I'm guessin'

187

that Hardman made you ride with his trail-trash. What's he got on you, Frank? Were you carryin' on with Lucy Andrews?'

'I tol' you once,' Brand said forcefully. 'She don't come into this.'

'But you were buyin' opium from Chang.'

'For Chris'sakes, Mr Stafford! I was givin' the opium to Hardman. He was makin' me buy it for him.'

Stafford felt the muscles across his shoulders relax. He filled his lungs with air. Tom Worley was going to walk away from that jail a free man. Brand had given him the answer he'd been hoping to get. He'd never suspected Hardman of taking opium. He'd worked too long with the man not to become aware of his vices. Being a slave to opium wasn't one of them. Hardman had been feeding Lucy Andrews with the drug and taking her to the cabin out in the wood. Again, the image of a young Swede flashed into his mind before he was able to push it away.

'Go back home, Frank, and start takin' over the Double B. Tell your father to get rid of Hardman. He's a snake an' a killer.'

'Mr Stafford, if I thought there was a chance I'd do that. But Hardman'll not shift. You don't know him.'

Stafford pushed himself off the table to

stand over Brand. 'I know Hardman better than you or anyone in Storm,' he said brusquely. 'I worked with him for almost two years. I'll tell you about Hardman. One day down in Kansas he crossed the line. A good man, my friend Amos Jackson, threatened to turn him in an' they had a fight.' Stafford breathed in deeply, remembering the day.

'Followin' day we were in a gunfight agin the no-goods we were trailin'. I ain't sure to this day what happened, but Amos ended up with a sidearm from Hardman. It blew up in Amos's face, killin' him.'

Stafford stopped suddenly. Brand's face had turned deathly white and for a moment Stafford thought he was about to topple from his chair.

Brand had his head down, muttering over and over again. 'Omigod, omigod, omigod!'

'What the hell's wrong?'

Brand lifted his head, a haunted expression in his eyes. 'We were out huntin'. Hardman, my brother Jamie, an' me. Jamie's sidearm blew up in his hand, killin' him.' He paused, swallowing rapidly. 'I'd given him the sidearm.'

'An' somewhere along the line you got it from Hardman,' Stafford said. He didn't need Brand's answer. It was written across the young man's face.

'Hardman said he'd swear to Pa that it was Jamie's own gun that killed him,' Brand said. 'I was to keep my mouth shut.' Brand looked over Stafford's shoulder, unseeing. 'I think Pa would've killed me.'

There were shouts and screams from the street penetrating the walls of Simpson's office but both Stafford and Brand ignored them.

'An' Hardman's been railroadin' you ever since,' Stafford said.

'Now you know why I'm quittin' the Double B,' Brand said.

Before Stafford could reply the door from the outer office was thrown open with a crash of wood against wood. Simpson stood at the door, sweat showing on his forehead.

'Come quick, Mr Stafford. That picture feller! He's been shot!'

Paying no further attention to Frank Brand, Stafford pushed past the lawyer and out onto the boardwalk. A knot of people, all of them looking down to the hardpack, were gathered in the centre of the street around a chestnut with a blazed face. An icy hand gripped Stafford's heart. Victoria's horse. He ran towards the group.

'Outa my way!'

He pushed his way through the townsfolk, to drop to one knee alongside Harry Galton who lay on his back, his eyes closed, blood staining his shirt and darkening the front of his jacket. A small man kneeled beside Galton, the sleeves of his shirt rolled up, cutting away Galton's clothing with a short knife. Doc Mayerling, Stafford guessed. Mayerling looked up at Stafford's arrival.

'He's been hurt bad,' he said.

'Harry, can you hear me?' Stafford said urgently, resisting the temptation to grab Galton by the shoulders. There was no response from Galton. Jesus Christ! Why had he ever allowed Galton to take such a gamble with Victoria and Miss Amy? If anything had happened to them he'd not be at peace with himself for the rest of his days.

'His eyes moved!' Stafford exclaimed. 'Harry! Can you hear me?'

Slowly Galton opened his eyes. 'Hardman,' he said weakly. ''Nother no-good.' A trickle of blood ran from the corner of his mouth. 'Taken the ladies,' he managed. His eyes closed.

Stafford clutched Mayerling's shoulder. 'A hundred dollars you save him, an' spend as much as it takes.'

He jumped to his feet, looking around at the townsfolk. He gaze fell on Mason, the councilman who'd spoken with him outside the livery. 'Tell Mackay I'm ridin' to the Double B.'

'An' I'm ridin' with Stafford,' a voice snapped behind him.

Stafford turned. 'C'mon, Frank!' he barked. 'We're gonna catch up with Hardman an' kill that sonovabitch!'

CHAPTER THIRTEEN

Stafford and Brand were maybe five miles from the Double B, their horses held to a lope after the hard gallop from Storm Creek, when Brand shouted out, 'Riders comin', Mr Stafford!'

Stafford reached for his Winchester, staring ahead. He swore under his breath. There was maybe a faint cloud of dust on the horizon but he was damned if he could make out riders. A picture of Mackay groping in his desk for his glasses flashed in his mind, and he swore again. He rested the barrel of his long gun across the saddle against the horn. If they were no-goods he'd see them before they got to gunshot range.

'I'm sure it's Pa!' Brand shouted.

Brand kicked his horse into a gallop drawing alongside Stafford who had spurred on his palomino after hearing Brand's shout. Both of them raced to meet the riders approaching them. He could now see Elisha Brand surrounded by his cowboys. Had they caught up with Hardman? Was Victoria safe? That's all Stafford wanted to hear.

'Pa! Pa!'

Brand shouted his greeting when he and Stafford were a few hundred yards from the group. They covered the distance at the gallop, bringing their horses to a sudden halt, pulling around their mounts' heads to draw close to Elisha Brand. Horses skittered across the ground as the two groups circled each other jostling for space.

'Mrs Ross an' Miss Amy. Are they safe?' Stafford shouted.

'Hardman and one of his men,' Elisha Brand called. 'They've taken them. We've searched west but seen nothing. We were heading east when we saw you. There's gonna be hard ridin' but we'll catch up with 'em.'

Brand appeared to take notice of his son for the first time. He raised a thumb to point behind him to the north. 'You get back to the ranch. Folks need you back there.' He turned in his saddle. 'Henderson! Pick one of the men to go back with Mr Frank.'

Frank Brand pushed his horse forward to close with his father. 'No, Pa! Not this time. Amy's my sister, an' my place is here. I'm ridin' with Mr Stafford.'

'Don't you defy me, boy.' The black shadows below the rancher's eyes began to show even darker. White lines stood out around his nose.

'No, Pa. That's enough. You ain't strong enough for this.'

'Who the hell–?' Brand rose in his stirrups.

'Take your son's advice, Brand.' Stafford interrupted the rancher. 'No sense in us bringin' back the ladies an' buryin' you the next day.'

Before the rancher could protest further Frank Brand turned to the tall lean man astride the grullo. 'Henderson! Pick a man to ride back with Mr Elisha. See he gets back in one piece.'

For a second or two Henderson hesitated, shooting a sidelong glance at Elisha Brand. Then his expression showed he had made his decision.

'Mr Frank's talkin' sense, boss.' Without waiting for Elisha to answer he swung around to face the younger Brand. 'Yessir, Mr Frank.' He turned his horse to the group of cowboys behind him. 'Downing! You ride back to the Double B with Mr Elisha.'

Stafford had expected a greater protest from Brand, but with a curse the rancher pulled round his horse's head as one of the

195

cowboys broke away from the group and moved alongside him. His head averted, as if to deny Downing's presence, Brand dug his heels into the sides of his horse and set off to the north without a backward glance.

'Henderson. You reckon your men could handle Hardman?'

'Reckon so, Mr Stafford. We ain't gun-fighters but there are still ten of us, an' we're all thinkin' o' Miss Amy.' Henderson frowned. 'You ain't comin' with us?'

'Me an' Mr Frank are goin' west agin. Hardman's as smart as a whip, an' he's mebbe holed up. If I'm wrong we'll catch up with you. OK. Let's get goin'!'

Henderson spurred his horse forward to take the lead ahead of the group of cowboys. Twenty yards and they were into a gallop heading east.

Stafford turned his mount. 'You can go with 'em, Frank. I could be wrong about this.'

Brand nodded. 'I know that. But we can catch up with Henderson if needs be.'

'OK. There's a cabin deep in a stand of cottonwoods. I'm guessin' that Hardman thinks he'll be safe until daybreak.'

Brand pulled down the brim of his hat further over his eyes. 'He touches a hair of

Amy's head an' he ain't gonna be safe for the rest of his life.'

Stafford reached the outer ring of cotton-woods, Brand a few paces behind him. For the last 500 yards they'd been on foot, having left the reins of their horses secured beneath a heavy rock.

As they'd approached the stand of trees Stafford had shown Brand a few hand signals. In the evening air even whispers would carry. If Hardman had holed up in the cabin he'd have posted his man among the trees to keep a lookout.

His Winchester held in his left hand, his Navy Colt held high in his right and ahead of him, Stafford began to work his way through the closely grown trunks of the cotton-woods. He reckoned he and Frank were to the east of the track he'd taken when Victoria had shown him the cabin.

The evening light was beginning to fade and, as the two men reached deeper into the woods, it became more difficult to see ahead. Stafford felt Brand's hand touch his shoulder. He turned to see Brand pointing over to his left. A glimmer of light shone between the trees. Was it Hardman or was it some traveller who'd stumbled across the cabin and found unexpected shelter? Stafford acknowledged Brand's signal and changed direction to slowly head for the light.

They continued to weave their way through the trees, Brand dropping back to five yards behind Stafford. Through the tangled branches of the trees the light from the cabin became clearer and Stafford judged they were no more than fifty yards from the cabin in the clearing.

The two shots rang out simultaneously, one of them so close it caused Stafford's ears to ring. Brand shouted with pain, and there was the sound of dried wood breaking as he crashed down. Stafford threw himself full length to the ground, his Winchester alongside him, his Colt at arm's length. An agonized whisper reached his ears.

'Bastard's got me, Luke.'

Keep your mouth shut! Stafford wanted to yell. If Hardman's man had heard Brand he'd know he could move in and finish the job. Stafford didn't move, waiting for Hardman's man to make a move. Where the hell was he? His eyes strained to penetrate the shadows, the shapes of trees momentarily taking on the shapes of men holding guns.

It was then, his ears straining, that he detected a sound that he'd heard maybe a hundred times but which never failed to raise the hairs on the back of his neck. Beyond the laboured breathing of Frank Brand came the slow rattle from a man's throat that is often heard at the point of death.

Stafford pushed himself up and, half-crouched, he weaved his way through the trees to reach Brand. The young man was on the ground, his back to a cottonwood. Between his teeth he was biting down on a length of wood he must have grabbed from the ground. Blood was seeping through a wound in his thigh around which Brand was tying tightly the neckerchief he'd worn.

'You got him, Frank.'

Brand spat out the wood. 'That bastard Hardman's gotta be in the cabin. You're gonna have to go in on your own.'

Stafford's thoughts raced. 'I come out an' I'm gonna shout your name.'

'You don't shout my name, an' I shoot everythin' I got.' Brand forced a grim smile. 'Get goin', Mr Stafford.'

In the dim light Stafford stared directly at the young man's face. Then with a brief nod he turned in the direction of the cabin. The light had been extinguished. He moved slowly through the trees, but his mind was racing. Hardman, he reckoned, would stay in the cabin, close to Victoria and Frank's sister. There was no way he could know how many men were near. Would it pay to try and bluff him? There was every chance that the dead sentry had seen Elisha Brand and his cowboys heading east. But would he have returned to the cabin and reported to Hardman?

He reached the inner ring of the cottonwoods and dropped to one knee, staring hard across the open clearing to the cabin. Nothing moved. The cabin door which he could barely make out in the fading light was closed. Was the shutter at the small opening to the right of the door open a few inches? Could he reach it before Hardman saw him moving across the open ground? Too far, he decided. Hardman would shoot him down before he was halfway to the cabin. For the moment he had no alternative. He'd got nothing to lose by trying a bluff.

'Jack Hardman!' Stafford shouted. 'It's Luke Stafford!'

There was a pause of a few seconds. Then, 'I hear you, Luke!'

'I got ten men with me, Jack. Give up the ladies an' we'll talk.'

'Guess you musta killed Hansen,' Hardman shouted. 'But you were always a lousy poker player. You're bluffin', Luke. I'm guessin' you're alone. Brand an' his men are long gone.'

Goddamnit! Hansen must have told Hardman what he'd seen. Stafford breathed in deeply, his mind turning over his options. He had to keep Hardman from hurting the women. That's if, he reminded himself grimly, he hadn't already done so. An icy hand clutched at his heart, as he realized he'd been assuming that both women were still alive. Hardman would need only one hostage to aid his escape. As if to answer his troubled mind a woman's voice shattered the silence.

'Luke!'

There was the sound of a slap that reached Stafford across the open ground, closely followed by a scream of pain. A scream of protest sounded in another voice. Victoria! She shouted his name, he was sure. And the other scream! Brand's daughter must also be alive.

'Jack! Let the ladies go,' Stafford shouted. 'We can talk this over.'

201

'Too late for that, Luke. I ain't gonna hang for that whore.'

'Listen! I don't give a damn about Lucy Andrews. I ain't paid to bring you in. Tom Worley's gonna walk outa jail tomorrow. That's what I'm about. Let the ladies go an' we'll keep our mouths shut. A few hours ridin' an' you'll be outa the territory.'

There was no immediate reply from Hardman. Stafford stayed on one knee, waiting. He'd played his best card, and he could only wait for Hardman's next move. He'd meant what he said about Hardman riding away. Worley was already out of trouble. The lives of Victoria and Miss Amy were worth a thousand like Hardman dangling from a rope.

'OK, Luke! We'll talk.'

Stafford felt a great wave of relief flood over him. He picked up his Winchester and stepped cautiously away from the trunk of the cottonwood.

'I'm comin' in, Jack.'

'You hold it there! I ain't finished yet. You gotta come in unarmed. An' don't fergit that knife you got tucked back o' your shirt.'

Stafford stood still. Was Hardman crazy to think he'd walk into the cabin without a weapon? Before he could shout his reply,

202

Hardman called out again.

'You get over here, Luke, like I said. Or I'm gonna start shootin' pieces off your woman.'

Stafford froze. Hardman would carry out his threat if he thought he'd get his way. Frantically, he racked his mind for options. Maybe he should just charge the cabin, blazing away, praying that Hardman's attention would be on him rather than the two women.

A shot rang out, closely followed by a woman's scream, then the sound of weeping. Oh, God! That was Victoria's voice he'd heard ring out, he was sure of it.

'I'm comin' in,' Stafford shouted. 'Just like you said, Jack.'

He threw down his long gun, unholstered his Colt and dropped it to the ground. Leaning back, he slid his hand below the collar of his shirt at the nape of his neck and withdrew the blade from its sheath. He dropped it to the ground alongside his Colt.

Filling his lungs with air he stepped away from the trees onto the open ground before the cabin. Would Hardman shoot him down before he'd reached the cabin? When they'd first worked together they'd got along fine. Maybe that was in his favour. He got closer to the cabin and was now able to make out the door.

'Hold it there, Luke!'

Stafford froze. The door to the cabin had opened a few inches. He heard a match rasp and then light flared from a lamp that he guessed was behind the door.

'OK. Make it slow.'

Stafford stepped into the cabin. Hardman must have been standing behind the door. The barrel of a sidearm pressed against the nape of Stafford's neck, hard enough for the gunsight to nick his skin. Hardman's hand felt at the nape of his neck, checking the sheath was empty. He ran his hand down Stafford's body checking that he was unarmed.

The pressure against Stafford's neck increased and he was prodded forward towards the centre of the cabin. The two women were standing alongside each other in a corner of the cabin. Victoria, her face as white as chalk, but with her head held high, stood with her arm around the shoulders of Amy Brand.

The younger woman had her head down, her chin touching the front of her dress, tears staining the front of a silk dress that shone in the light thrown by the lamp. Around her shoulders was a delicate stole made from fine lace. Stafford saw, too, that Victoria wore her special riding habit given to her by the Englishwoman. His surprise faded when he remembered Galton's request that they should wear good clothes for the photograph.

'Welcome to the party, Luke,' Hardman said.

Stafford ignored him. 'Has he hurt you, Victoria?'

She shook her head, tightening her arm around Amy Brand.

'I'm fortunate to have my companion.'

'Tol' you I was a better poker player, Luke. I ain't hurt the ladies.' Hardman leered across the cabin. 'Maybe a slap or two.'

Stafford turned. 'You know my word's good. We'll ride outa here, an' you'll be clear.'

Hardman held his sidearm loosely down by his left side but Stafford knew better to make a move. He'd seen Hardman in action too many times to be that stupid. He stood still waiting for Hardman's response.

'Afore you ride outa here,' Hardman said. 'You gonna tell me how you knew it was me who killed Lucy Andrews.'

'Mackay solved it for me,' Stafford said. 'He leaned over his desk to cut through a parcel for Tom Worley. He's right-handed. A left-hander's cut from behind follows a different line. I saw the cut on the gal's throat.'

Hardman glanced down at the sidearm alongside his left hip. A grim smile flickered at the corner of his mouth. 'You were always smart, Luke, I'll give you that. I remember that business down in Kansas with old Amos Jackson. You almos' figured that out. Told 'em in Chicago all about it, I recall.'

Stafford hoped his face was in shadow. He knew then that Hardman intended to kill him. Hardman had never been before a judge for killing old Amos. But it had cost him his job with Pinkerton's. Overnight, Hardman had become just another gun for hire, scrabbling for crumbs from the tables of wealthy men.

Stafford became conscious of Victoria staring directly at him. To hell with it! He wasn't going to let her see him begging for his life. There was a good chance that Hardman would let her go. Two women would slow him down, and Hardman liked them young.

'You killed Jamie Brand the same way,' Stafford said. 'What was that about, Jack? Was he carryin' on with Lucy Andrews, an' you wanted her?'

Hardman's coarse laughter filled the cabin. 'You're really somethin', Luke, you know that?' He gestured with his sidearm. 'He was gonna have Brand fire me, I reckon.' He shrugged. 'So I took his woman and this cabin he'd been usin'.' His lips pulled back from his teeth. 'Made it look like Brand's whelp done it.'

Hardman raised his sidearm, and pointed it directly at Victoria Ross. 'You! Outside! Me an' your man friend are gonna follow you.'

Stafford felt his flesh go cold. Could Victoria escape if he had time to shout that she should run towards the trees? Victoria took her arm from around the younger woman and moved towards the door. She would be close to him for a precious moment.

He knew what Hardman intended. He was going to shoot them both out of sight of Amy Brand. He was going to keep her for himself. A night with her, and she'd obey him like a whipped cur. He took a step as Victoria moved towards him.

A shot rang out, a brief flash of light flickering beyond the partly open shutter. The cabin was plunged into blackness. Stafford, sucking in air to hold his breath, curled one arm around Victoria's waist and dragged them both to the floor. His one hand slammed against her mouth preventing her from crying out, as together he rolled them towards the rear wall of the cabin. His hand groped beneath her skirt, sliding over slippery silk that covered warm soft flesh.

Three shots rang out, the reports so close that they stung Stafford's ears, the bitter smell of powder assaulting his nostrils. Hardman, unable to see in the blackness, was firing his sidearm indiscriminately. Frank Brand had given them a chance but was it too late?

Stafford held Victoria behind him, praying that Amy Brand was out of the line of fire. Could he move without endangering Victoria? His heart was beating so strongly he thought it might break through his chest. Where the hell was Hardman? He swung his head from left to right attempting to penetrate the blackness. There! For an instant Hardman showed his outline against the opening in the shutter.

Stafford pulled the trigger. Five .22 slugs from Victoria's Ladies Companion slammed into Hardman. None had sufficient velocity to smash through the back of Hardman's head. Instead, they tore through flesh and gristle, ricocheting from the bones of his skull through bloody pulp and shredding the soft tissue of his brain. Hardman was dead before his body hit the floor.

CHAPTER FOURTEEN

Stafford stood alongside Tom Worley in the back yard of Worley's new clapboard at the edge of Storm Creek. On the ground before them was spread out a large map of the area showing the homesteads. Grouped on the other side of the map stood the ex-soldiers peering down at the long cane that Worley was moving over the map.

'For the plan to work,' Worley said, 'Theo Morgan will have to move from his homestead to here.' He moved the cane across the paper. 'That will give you a continuous line of homesteads.'

'I can't do that, Mr Worley!' Morgan exclaimed. 'I been workin' that place for over a year.'

'Hold your fire, Mr Morgan. I haven't finished.' Worley moved the cane again. 'You'll see that each of your homesteads will then back onto each of the homesteads that have been abandoned.'

'Driven off 'em, you mean.'

The men turned to stare hard at Frank

210

Brand who was standing a few yards away from the group, leaning on the stout stick that took the weight off his injured leg.

'Give Mr Worley a chance to explain,' Stafford said sharply.

The men turned back to face Worley. 'Go ahead, Mr Worley,' Joe Bagley said.

'This week ten thousand saplings are coming into town. They're paid for, and you can pay me back over time. On the stretch of each abandoned homestead you plant the saplings,' Worley said.

'An' why the heck should we do that, Mr Worley? An' owe you money? Don't make sense,' called out Jenkins.

Worley grinned. 'Because the Timber Culture Act of '73 states that if you plant trees you double the size of your homestead. Each man will also own the empty homestead adjoining his.'

For a moment there was stunned silence. Then the men broke into noisy chatter, laughing, and digging each other in the ribs, congratulating each other on their good fortune.

'Hold on!' Joe Bagley's voice rang out over the hullabaloo. 'What's Theo Morgan reckon to all this?'

The men fell silent, all looking at Morgan,

who was thoughtfully stroking his beard. 'I guess it's OK,' he said slowly. 'Seein' as I'm gonna double my spread. Darned shame 'bout the cabin an' the barn though, an' there's the early plantin'. I ain't sure I can make it through the winter.'

'S'pose three men came over with ploughs to your new place while the rest planted trees,' suggested Stafford.

Frank Brand moved closer. 'Say I send men over from the Double B with lots o' wagons. You can take the whole barn an' cabin, you want.' He looked steadily at the ex-soldiers. 'I aim to be runnin' the Double B for a long time. We're gonna be neighbours. Makes sense we get along.'

The men exchanged looks, their expressions indicating they thought Brand's words made good sense. They looked expectantly at Morgan.

'If I got help to get started agin then it's fine with me,' Morgan said.

There were whoops of pleasure from the men. Stafford decided it was a good time to leave. 'I'm goin' to the schoolhouse,' he told Worley.

'This shouldn't take long,' Worley said. 'But I need to finish here.'

'I'll pick you up in the buggy,' Brand said.

Stafford found Victoria at her table in the schoolroom, her head bent over the paper in front of her. She looked up as he walked halfway down the room and sat on one of the tables, his feet on the back of a stool. He smiled as he saw her eyes widen with surprise.

'My, oh my! Haven't you changed!'

Stafford laughed aloud. He ran his hands down the front of his grey Prince Albert and touched the material of his pants. 'Stage got in early this morning with these.' His eyes sought her approval.

'I think they're perfect.' She leaned slightly to her left, a smile dancing around her lips as she made a great play of staring at his hip. 'Maybe a little underdressed?'

Stafford grinned. 'I reckon a Colt might be too much for a council meeting.' He paused, his grin fading. 'I been thinkin' 'bout what Kenney at the Majestic tol' me last night. Hardman had one of his men reserve that room in Miss Amy's name so he musta been plannin' to kill Lucy Andrews from then. I reckon she musta told Hardman they were finished after she got the letter from Chicago Mrs Andrews tol' me about.'

'And he planned to get rid of Tom at the

same time.'

'Two targets for one shot. The same way he killed Jamie Brand an' got power over Frank. I tol' you he was smart.'

He pushed back the front of his coat, keen to change the subject. 'You don't think the silk vest is a mite fancy for Storm?'

'It's fine.'

'I was just wonderin',' he said, and paused a moment. 'Anyways, the stage brought in the letter for me from Boston.'

'Oh yes?' There was a little catch in Victoria's voice.

'They tol' me when I get tired of marriage and small-town life I can have my job back.'

'Oh!'

'So you're sure you know what you're doin'?'

'I'm sure. Oh, yes, I'm sure.'

Stafford's smile faded as his face grew serious. 'Then there's something I need to tell you afore next week. Somethin' you need to know about me.'

Victoria caught his change of mood immediately. 'What is it, Luke?'

Stafford breathed in deeply. No matter how many times he'd mentally rehearsed this moment it was going to be more difficult than he'd imagined.

'Lots of brave men died alongside me during the War,' he said slowly, marshalling his thoughts. 'I shall remember some of them until the day I die. But for different reasons there's one I can't forget.' He looked away from Victoria, staring through the schoolhouse window.

'His name was Carlson, a big fair Swede, about the age of Frank Brand. An' from the day he joined us he was trouble. He'd fall asleep at the wrong time, neglect his clothing and equipment, fail to clean his weapons.'

Stafford took another deep breath. 'Joe Bagley was good with the men. He still is. A velvet glove in an iron fist. I ordered him to railroad Carlson twenty-four hours a day. Carlson's life was to be made hell until he came into line. Joe did exactly what I'd ordered. But Carlson failed to improve.' Stafford shook his head, still puzzled after many years. 'Yet Carlson was popular with the other men. I could never figure it out.'

He forced himself to look back at Victoria. 'Anyways, a coupla months before Petersburg we were holed up near a place called Dragget's Wood. The night we got the order to move Carlson walked into the wood and blew his brains out.' Stafford's mouth set.

'To this day I reckon I sent that boy to his death.'

The silence in the schoolroom stretched across time as seconds ticked by. Victoria and Stafford remained looking across the room at each other. Finally, Victoria spoke.

'Is that why you gave Frank Brand a chance?'

Surprised, Stafford slid from the desk to stand in the middle of the room.

'Frank's got nothing to do with it.'

Before Victoria could respond, the school-room door opened. 'What's that I've nothing to do with?'

Stafford turned to see Frank Brand at the door, leaning on his stick and sweeping off his hat with a dramatic gesture.

'Howdy, Victoria.' He turned to Stafford, screwing up his eyes. 'You sure take some gettin' used to dressed fancy like that.'

Stafford grinned, hoping the awkwardness he felt wasn't showing on his face. 'We were just sayin' you got nothin' else to think about than Tom Worley marryin' Miss Amy.' He paused. 'Was everythin' OK after I left?'

'Sure did. We gotta deal. Dry season, an' I can drive my stock over Morgan's old place to the water. They're jumpin' 'round like jack-rabbits over takin' the abandoned

216

homesteads. I reckon those saplings gonna be planted by the end o' summer.'

'How's your pa takin' it?' Stafford knew that Worley had been out to the ranch a couple of days before to explain to Elisha Brand what was being planned.

'Doc Mayerling tol' him if he didn't accept times are changin' he'd be dead in six months.' Frank grinned. 'He's sittin' on the porch tellin' anyone he can catch how he fought the Indians in the early days.'

'But the Shoshone have always been friendly.' Victoria exclaimed.

'He thinks we don't know that.' Brand took the gold timepiece from the pocket in his vest. 'Amy's gone to the Majestic with Tom. They'll be waiting for us.'

The buggy drew up outside the store still bearing the sign announcing that Galton had worked with the famous Civil War photographer Mathew Brady. Stafford handed the reins to Victoria.

'Drive down to the Majestic and wait for us there. We'll be along in a few minutes.'

The two men stood watching as Victoria flicked the reins and the buggy moved forward. Then they turned and went up the steps to the store.

'Harry! You still here?' Stafford called at the open door.

Inside, the rear door of Galton's store opened. Galton appeared in the doorway seated in a chair on wheels being pushed by the young man Stafford had seen in Mackay's office.

'Howdy Luke, Frank.' Galton smacked the armrests of the chair with the flat of his open palm. 'Fancy, eh? Josh Andrews had it brought up from Cheyenne for me.'

'How you feelin', Harry?' Stafford asked.

'Doc Mayerling reckons I'll be outa this contraption by the end o' the year, an' walkin' by next springtime.' He jerked a thumb behind him. 'I'm lucky I got Tommy here lookin' after me. Wants to be a sheriff some day an' he's learning the tricks o' the trade.'

'You reckon makin' pictures gonna be useful?' Frank Brand asked doubtfully.

Harry exchanged looks with Stafford. 'Yeah, could be,' he said. 'But that ain't all I'm teachin' him, Frank.' Galton looked around before shaking his head. 'Too small, I guess. Let's get outside. Tommy's got somethin' to show you.'

Tommy pushed at the chair, and the four of them went out onto the boardwalk. Galton waited until a couple of townsfolk heading for the Majestic had passed with a cheerful greeting.

'OK, Frank. Take a swing at Tommy,' Galton said.

'I can't do that!'

'Sure you can. Go ahead.'

Brand still hesitated, but seeing the three were waiting on him, he stepped forward. 'If you're real sure.' Brand faced Tommy. 'I don't want to hurt you, Tommy.'

Tommy nodded. 'That's OK, Mr Brand.'

'Here goes,' said Frank.

His fist curled towards the side of Tommy's chin. Stafford wasn't sure what happened next. Tommy appeared to spin around, fling himself forward, and roll across the boards without any apparent impact on his shoulder. In an instant he was on his feet facing Frank, his hand held forward as if holding a sidearm.

'*Samurai!*' he exclaimed.

'Jumpin' rattlesnakes!' Brand waved his stick in mid-air. 'What's that? A Comanche war-cry?'

'*Samurai*,' Galton explained. 'Old warriors in Japan. Two of 'em fled to Frisco when the *Samurai* were broken up in '68. I was the only round-eye who'd talk with 'em.' He turned his head to peer through the open door at the clock above his desk. 'We better get goin'. It's almost noon.'

The townsfolk got to their feet and cheered when Galton, pushed by Tommy, led the little group into the big room at the Majestic. Mason, the councilman who'd spoken with Stafford several days before stood on a small platform at the end of the room. He held up his hand for quiet as Stafford and the rest took their seats at the front alongside Tom Worley and Amy Brand.

'You all know why we're here,' Mason said loudly, making sure everyone could hear. 'Storm Creek has had its troubles these last days. But brave men have brought peace back to our town. So I'm gonna leave it to the sheriff to tell you what's happening.'

Mackay left his seat near the platform and stepped up to face the room. He tucked his thumbs into the belt around his prominent stomach and coughed to clear his throat.

'I been sheriff o' Storm Creek for nigh on ten years,' he said, his face reddening at the outburst of cheering that greeted his words. He looked down at Stafford before he held up a hand for quiet.

'I never thought the day would come when I had a Pinkerton man for a deputy. An' you folk oughta know how lucky you are.' Again cheering broke out. Ex-Pinkerton man, thought Stafford, as Victoria squeezed his hand.

'Mind you, it's only gonna be for a month,' Mackay continued, when he could make himself heard. 'Then I'm ridin' off into the sunset.'

'You mean to that clapboard back o' the livery stable?' A voice came from the back of the room.

'Yeah, I guess I do,' Mackay said, when the laughter had died away. 'Anyways,' he went on, 'here's the feller who's gonna be your sheriff to say somethin'.'

Upturned faces looked expectantly in Stafford's direction as he got to his feet, and stepped up to the platform. For a fleeting moment, looking at the calm decent faces of the townsfolk, he wondered how he'd settle to being a small-town sheriff. Yes, there'd been dangerous times as a Pinkerton agent. More than once he'd been lucky to walk away alive. But the money had been good, and he'd always felt he was doing something worthwhile. How would he feel about collecting taxes, pulling drunken cowboys out of the saloon on a Saturday night, chasing young brats who'd cut school? Then Amos

Jackson's words came back to him.

'Remember, Luke, nobody gets to be a gunfighter for ever.'

As Stafford scanned the room, seeing his friends, the townsfolk, the old soldiers of his regiment, and even a few cowboys from the Double B, he realized he could have no finer task than upholding the law for this small town of a territory that one day would surely achieve statehood. Stafford looked down at the sweet face of the woman who in a few days would be his wife. Then once more he scanned the room.

'Thank you for electing me,' he said. 'I aim to serve this town for as long and I hope as honourably as Mr Mackay.' He paused for a moment.

'I give you my word.'

The publishers hope that this book has given you enjoyable reading. Large Print Books are especially designed to be as easy to see and hold as possible. If you wish a complete list of our books please ask at your local library or write directly to:

Dales Large Print Books
Magna House, Long Preston,
Skipton, North Yorkshire.
BD23 4ND

This Large Print Book, for people
who cannot read normal print,

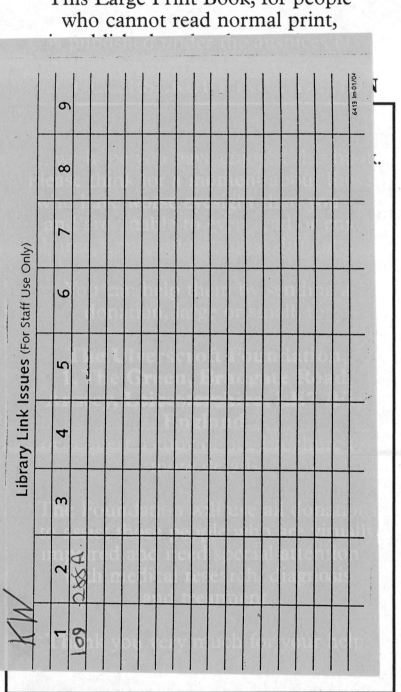